PETER CORRIS was born in Stawell, Victoria, in 1942. He has worked as a lecturer and researcher in history as well as a freelance writer and journalist, specialising in sports writing. He has written thrillers, a social history of prizefighting in Australia, quiz books, radio and television scripts, and the historical novels *The Gulliver Fortune*, *Naismith's Dominion*, *The Brothers Craft*, and *Wimmera Gold*. He is also the co-author of *Fred Hollows, An Autobiography*.

The Reward is the twenty-first in his successful series of books about Sydney-based private eye Cliff Hardy.

CW00606416

THE REWARD

A Cliff Hardy novel

by

Peter Corris

BANTAM BOOKS
SYDNEY • AUCKLAND • TORONTO • NEW YORK • LONDON

THE REWARD
A BANTAM BOOK

First published in Australia and New Zealand in 1997 by Bantam

Copyright © Peter Corris 1997

National Library of Australia.
Cataloguing-in-Publication Entry

Corris, Peter, 1942– .
The reward: Cliff Hardy stories.

ISBN 0 7338 0070 X.

I. Title.

A 823.3

Bantam books are published by

Transworld Publishers (Aust) Pty Limited
15–25 Helles Avenue, Moorebank, NSW 2170

Transworld Publishers (NZ) Limited
3 William Pickering Drive, Albany, Auckland

Transworld Publishers (UK) Limited
61–63 Uxbridge Road, Ealing, London W5 5SA

Bantam Doubleday Dell Publishing Group Inc
1540 Broadway, New York, New York 10036

Cover design by Noel Pennington/Design Bite
Cover photograph by Jack Sarafian
Typeset by Midland Typesetters, Victoria
Printed by McPherson's Printing Group, Victoria

10 9 8 7 6 5 4 3 2 1

Thanks to Paul Abraham, Jean Bedford,
Rebekah Donaldson, Sofya Gollan, Tom Kelly,
Tania Sourdin

1

'Do you remember Ramona Beckett, Hardy?'

'I remember her,' I said.

'Perhaps you also remember that her family offered a reward for information leading to the arrest and conviction of whoever was responsible for her death. This was about two years after she disappeared, and that's fifteen fucking years ago.'

I shrugged. 'If you say so.'

'Am I right in thinking that you had something to do with her?'

The man who'd asked the question was Barry White, an ex-cop, ex-private detective, ex-night-club bouncer, ex just about anything in that line you could think of. He was middle class, university educated and had made Detective Sergeant pretty quickly, but he'd resigned from the force just ahead of a corruption charge. Like me, he'd lost his PEA licence for breaches of the regulations. I'd regained mine fairly easily and quickly on the basis of a previously good record and the recommendations of police officers and others whose integrity was unquestioned at a time when a lot of questioning was going on.

White hadn't been so lucky. The only cops he knew were as corrupt as he was and were leaving the force under clouds or to go behind bars. He was a big, strong man, or had been, and he'd looked pretty formidable outside a nightclub for a while. But the booze softened and slowed him and people who like to start trouble in those places these days have learned martial arts tricks that can make an old thumper like Barry look silly. Me too, for that matter. So he'd slipped down a few more notches. When he turned up at my office that Monday morning I thought he might be scrounging for work. He wasn't.

'I knew her, yes.'

Ramona was a rich, spoiled young woman who wanted to be the first female Premier of New South Wales. She did a sociology degree at Sydney and, after blooding herself in university politics and local government, she decided that blackmail was the way to go. She set about seducing politicians and influential people with the aim of getting leverage on them to put her where she wanted to be in politics. One of her victims had had the guts to come to me professionally and I'd helped him.

'We'll get to that. The unusual thing about this reward,' White said, 'is that the money was well invested and has accrued interest. The amount on offer now stands at over one million dollars.'

'I didn't know that.'

'It's a long time ago. People forget. But no-one was ever charged with Beckett's murder and the reward is still available, although her father's dead now. You might remember that her mother was much younger. Mrs Beckett is still very much alive and at last report was still keen to see justice done.'

I didn't much like the smell of this. 'It's nearly seventeen years ago, Barry,' I said. 'Sure, I was around when it all happened, where were you?'

He grinned and as it changed expression the high-coloured face showed the marks of booze and fists and late nights. He wouldn't have been much over forty and he looked sixty. He took out a packet of Drum tobacco and probed in it for the papers. 'You mind?'

I said I didn't but I did, a bit. I used to roll them myself and I still missed the taste of the tobacco, especially the first three or four smokes on a clean palate, but I didn't miss the cough and the short wind. Still, the smell was good and there was no law against me enjoying that. He rolled the smoke expertly and lit it with a match which he put in his jacket pocket. He wore a business shirt, not too clean, a tie likewise, a double-breasted blazer with one gold button missing, grey trousers and black shoes that had just had a shine. He sported a fresh haircut and shave and I could smell the lotions. I hadn't seen him for a while but what I'd heard of him was that his marriage was washed up and that he was living in a room in Chippendale. Clearly, he'd spruced himself up to see me. I was suspicious rather than flattered.

He blew smoke towards the window where a little more grime wouldn't hurt. I had the office painted and the windows cleaned a year ago when I was given a two-year lease. It looked all right for a while but somehow lately it'd slipped back.

'I was there, too,' White said. 'I was a probationary D at the 'Loo.'

'What's this about, Barry?'

'Fuck, what d'you think? It's about the money, of course. I've got a line on who knocked Beckett.'

'Oh, yeah? And who was that?'

He laughed through an exhalation of smoke and the cough caught him like a hard right to the ribs. He doubled over and his face turned purple as he fought the spasm.

'Jesus, Barry,' I said. 'You're holding a full hand for a heart attack.'

'I know,' he gasped, fighting for breath. When he finally sucked some air in he said, 'I'm just about fucked if I don't get this money. I've got high blood pressure, a touch of emphysema and a crook liver. They reckon I can pull out of it if I stop drinking and smoking, lose weight and eat lettuce. If I can get the money I'll do it. I'll go to one of those health farms in the fucking Blue Mountains and drink mineral water and be a good boy. It'll be worth it. Kicking shit the way I am now, I'd just as soon be out at Rookwood.'

I nodded. I could understand that. It's easy to eat healthily if you can afford asparagus and chicken fillets. A good bottle of wine won't do the damage of a slab of beer. Trouble was, that line of thought made me feel like a drink and it was only four o'clock in the afternoon—two hours before my self-imposed starting time. He went into a coughing fit again and while I waited for him to recover I tried to remember what dealings I'd had with him before. There wasn't much, a bit of a brush when he was extorting from a madam named Ruby Thompson who was a friend and I asked him to lay off. He got even by verballing a client of mine who was probably guilty anyway but deserved a second chance.

He got his breath back and looked at the cigarette he'd put in the ashtray. He reached over and snuffed it out. Maybe he could rehabilitate himself after all.

'OK, OK, I'd forgotten your sense of humour. Try not to make me laugh, Hardy. I could drop dead on you.'

I was thinking he could drop dead for all I cared, but I knew that wasn't quite true. I had ambivalent feelings about Ramona Beckett, but my feelings about a million dollars were pretty straightforward.

'The way I heard it, you screwed her, literally and otherwise.'

'No comment.'

'Come on, Hardy. I'm lining up a hundred thousand fucking dollars for you. I need to know how close you got to her.'

While I didn't have White's health problems, things weren't getting easier. I was pushing fifty and the private detective business, like everything else, was rapidly being taken over by computers. Process-serving was being done by E-mail and fax, money was moved electronically rather than in briefcases, and there were big agencies specialising in finding lost kids, de-bugging offices and protecting men in suits. I didn't have any life insurance and the superannuation the government was obliging me to pay myself wouldn't keep me in red wine and secondhand books if I stopped earning. I *had* to be interested in a hundred thousand bucks. There were a lot of questions in my head but it was best to play along, for now.

'You knew what her line was, did you?'

'Not really. Tell me.'

I told him. 'This bloke she was blackmailing came to me for help and we set her up. Sort of biter bit thing. I pretended to be a bigwig, a lawyer who controlled the preselection for a safe Liberal seat. She arranged her usual deal—the drinks, the fuck in her Potts Point flat, the video camera. Only she was a solo operator by necessity and couldn't keep her finger on everything. I had help. I had someone swipe the video and substitute another one. I taped her when she came to me with the pitch. Then I turned the tables on her—told her I'd send the video to her dad and give the tape to the cops and the papers. She backed off after that, but she might have done it again, just being more careful. I don't know. She went missing . . . oh, about a year after that, maybe less.'

White nodded. 'I get it.'

I'd tried to tell it matter-of-factly, but it hadn't been like that at all. Ramona Beckett was hell on wheels, tall, dark, thin with sexual energy in every gesture. She ate like a wharfie and was a junior gymnastics champion who ran fifteen kilometres every day. She had a fast metabolism but her touch was strangely cold. She got by on five or six hours' sleep, she read a lot of books and liked to wear black leather, the way she had the night I turned the tables on her. She was a living, breathing contradiction—a feminist, a reactionary, a corrupter and an idealist. She genuinely believed that she could improve life in the state for everyone, if only she could acquire the power to do it. She ended up hating me, of course, but I couldn't say I had the same feeling for her. I got a tissue from a pocket pack in the desk drawer and blew my nose. Clear the sinuses and you can clear a lot more besides. 'Any number of people could have had reason to kill her,' I said.

'Including the guy you worked for?'

I shrugged. 'Who knows? Maybe. Maybe he didn't tell me the whole story. But he's definitely not a candidate to bring in the reward on because he's dead.'

Out came the tobacco again and the brown-stained fingers rolled the cigarette just as deftly as before. He looked at it, burred over the ends, smoothed out the wrinkles, tapped it on his thumbnail and didn't light it. 'Better not,' he said. 'You might make me laugh again.'

'I'll try not to. Why don't you try not beating about the bush? You said you had a line.'

White leaned forward across the desk. His teeth were bad and his breath was worse. He was sweating too and there was a stale odour coming from his clothes. 'The word is, it was a kidnapping. There was a ransom note that got suppressed.'

2

That got my attention. Until very recently there were any number of cops and lawyers and magistrates and politicians in Sydney who acted as if none of the laws applied to them; seventeen years ago it was even worse. 'That's interesting, Barry,' I said. 'Tell me more.'

He eased back in his chair. 'Are you in?'

'Come on, I'd have to know a lot more than that. And in for what? You said a hundred grand.'

'That's right. Ten per cent. That's generous. I'd have to split the reward with at least three other people.'

'Who?'

He shook his head. 'I need a commitment.'

'And I get a five hundred dollar retainer and two hundred a day plus expenses.'

'Do I look like I've got that sort of money? You'd have to work on a contingency basis.'

It's a natural reaction to place some confidence in a person with a decent vocabulary and a reasonable command of grammar, but in Barry White's case the impulse had to be fought against. As I say, he was well educated and no-one ever called him dumb, but he was corrupt and devious, or had been, and I've never known adversity to straighten anyone out. 'I don't think so, Barry. No.'

He gave that grin again which must have been appealing when he was in better condition. He squirmed bulkily in the chair and took a thin wallet from his hip pocket. 'It was worth a try, Hardy.' He took seven one hundred dollar notes from the wallet and laid them on the desk. 'This buys me one day, right? The retainer's returnable if you back out.'

His eyes were faintly bloodshot and it clearly hurt him to part with the money. That he was doing it meant something, but what? 'That's right, *if* I take you on. You're not a good bet, Barry. You verballed blokes and planted drugs on women and took kickbacks till you forgot what job you were supposed to be doing.'

'All that's true,' he said. 'I was a fucking idiot. I thought I was too smart to get caught. Do you know what I did with all that money? I drank and ate and fucked it away. That's how dumb I was. I've got nothing, Hardy. No wife, no kids, no house, no reputation, no pride. All I've got is this one chance. Have you ever been down to one chance?'

'Not quite.'

'But close?'

I thought about how it had been when Cyn left me, coldly removing every single item she'd owned and breaking a lot of those we'd owned jointly. I thought about the alcoholic slide I'd gone into when Glen Withers married her policeman and the nice, structured life I'd had had fallen apart like a house of cards. And it was my fault. 'Pretty close.'

His eyes darted around the room, taking in the dirty windows, the dust on the fax machine and the top of the filing cabinet, the peanut shells in the waste-paper basket. 'You're not exactly setting the world on fire yourself, are you?'

If we'd been in a boxing ring, you'd have to have called the round about even. I was tired of sparring. I knew I wanted a crack at the hundred grand, I just didn't want to do it completely on his terms. 'Why d'you need me, Barry? You were a cop and a PEA. You know the ropes. You've got some information, some contacts, some leads. You know how to talk to people. Why're you here?'

If he knew he had me, he didn't show it. He finally brought the rollie up to his mouth and lit it, again putting the match in his pocket. It made me wonder if he'd been inside where they do little things like saving matches to play cards with. He drew on the smoke judiciously. 'I haven't got the resources,' he said. 'I haven't got a car or a mobile or an answering machine. I haven't got any decent clothes and most of all I haven't got the contacts. This is going to mean talking to cops and lawyers and journos. You can do it, I can't. There's a few things we can do together, but not much. That's why I need someone. I'm not going to piss in your pocket, Hardy, but I know you don't rip people off. That's why I need *you*. What d'you say?'

The lawyers are all doing it, so why not the PEAs? I negotiated a contract with Barry White on a contingency basis. I was to get 10 per cent of whatever reward money he recovered, my cut to come off the top. How he divided up the remainder was his business. I had the option to work on other matters simultaneously and to pull out of the arrangement at any time after the first week. This meant I was giving him six days' credit. Give a little, take a little. He signed with a flourish.

'Shit, I need a drink,' he said.

'I'll shout you one in a minute. First things first. Where does the information about the ransom note come from?'

White had finished his cigarette without choking and he made another one. 'Does the name Leo Grogan mean anything to you?'

'I don't think so.'

'He was a Homicide Squad D. Good cop, but the grog got to him and he was invalided out. I was having a few drinks with him a week or so ago, just shooting the shit, you know. The Beckett case came up. Leo was pissed, of course. He was on the team that looked into it. He reckoned certain people took certain sums of money to suppress a ransom note.'

'That's vague,' I said. 'What people? And who paid up?'

'That's where I played it smart. Leo hasn't got any time for me. If I showed an interest he'd clam up for sure. I sounded him out about the reward. He thought it lapsed when the old man died.'

'So?'

'I told you there were things we could do together. This is one of them. We have to go to Grogan, get him oiled just right and tell him how things stand. We cut him in for a third if everything works out.'

'What if he won't play?'

'I happen to know he's drawing a disability pension he's not entitled to and that he's got assets he hasn't declared. If he gets stroppy . . .'

So there it was. Cyn always said that the people I associated with made me violent, insensitive and untrustworthy by osmosis. I resisted the idea but here was a good chance to test it. Barry White had his copy of the contract in his pocket and mine was in my filing cabinet. I could always pull out of this if it got too sticky, couldn't I? I went to the nearest pub with White and bought him three schooners of old with his money while I drank a couple of middies of light. The beer didn't seem to affect him until someone spilled a drink that splashed his newly pressed trousers.

'You black cunt,' White said. He lurched towards the man, a stocky Maori in singlet, jeans and work boots.

'What did you say?' The Maori put the drinks he was carrying down and set himself.

White threw a punch that missed and tipped him off balance. The Maori had been ready to punch but White's stumble forced him to hold back. That gave me time to move in, grab the Maori's cocked right and jam it up behind his back. I pushed him a couple of steps so that he was up against a wall and couldn't get any leverage to swing back with his left. He was strong but when you're in that position strong doesn't help, any movement hurts like hell.

'He's drunk, mate,' I said in the Maori's ear. 'And he's a sick man. Look at him. You hit him and you're likely to kill him. He's an ex-copper, as well. You don't need that kind of trouble.'

'OK, brother, OK,' the Maori said. 'D'you want a go?'

'I've seen all the blood and broken glass I need to see for the rest of my life. Just let it be.' I released him and stepped away quickly, deciding to kick at his right knee if he was still belligerent. He glared at me and maybe the broken nose and scars convinced him.

'You're lucky you've got a sharp mate, pisspot,' he said to White as he wrapped his big hands around the drinks. He walked away to the other end of the bar.

White was dabbing at his damp pants with a dirty handkerchief. 'Good team, Hardy.'

'Fuck you,' I said. 'I ought to tear that bloody contract up.'

'You won't.'

He was right. The small confrontation with the Maori made me realise how much I was relying on old tricks like armlocks and new ones like staying sober. If I wasn't quite over the hill I was certainly nearing the top, and a six-figure score would help me to face the summit with much greater equanimity. White didn't know where Leo

Grogan lived, but he knew where he'd be at 10 a.m. the following day—in the bar of the Cleveland Hotel in Chippendale. White himself lived in a room in a boarding house in Rose Street and I agreed to give him a lift home. We walked to where I park the Falcon in Upper Forbes Street and White sneered as I undid the club lock.

'You're in the fucking Dark Ages, Hardy. I used to have a Commodore with one of the first automatic locking systems.' He held up an imaginary remote control. 'Press a button. Beep, beep, and you're sweet.'

I put the lock on the floor at his feet, started the motor and didn't say anything. He reached down, a bit unsteadily, picked up the device and examined it.

'Piece of shit. I knew blokes who could knock the lock out of that in two seconds flat.' He dropped the lock on the floor and got out his tobacco.

'Not in the car,' I said. 'You're talking about policemen, I suppose?'

'Yeah, of course.'

'I know people who can take out any car alarm system ever made and start the motor from the pavement.'

That shut him up. He slumped down in his seat and I could sense the good feeling the beer had given him already ebbing away. The question was, did he come up passive or aggressive? We drove down William Street. Daylight saving had just ended and a bit after seven o'clock the light was fading and the girls were beginning to emerge. White gazed out at them, and I glanced at him to gauge his response.

'Jesus,' he said. 'Will you take a look at that.'

A six-foot transvestite or transsexual stood on the kerb outside a luxury car showroom. She had long, shimmering silver-blonde hair and wore a halter top, miniskirt and thigh-high boots to match.

'Her dick's probably bigger than yours.'

'What's the difference?' he muttered. 'A hole's a fucking hole.'

I dropped him in Rose Street opposite a three-storey terrace that would fetch a fortune when it stopped being a dosshouse. I've seen plenty of those places in my time; the metho bottles in the backyard can outnumber the sweet sherry flagons. White had wound his window down and stuck his face out on the drive in an effort to clear his head. He climbed stiffly from the car and leaned through the open window.

'I'm broke, Hardy. That seven hundred was all I had. Can you lend me a few bucks?'

'Sure,' I said. 'Just tell me who staked you in the first place.'

'You're a bastard.'

'I have to be. I deal with them every day. Don't lie to me, Barry. The way things are, every word we exchange is important.'

'A woman. I've made her certain promises.'

'She's an idiot.'

'Maybe, but she doesn't think so.'

Human beings are hard to understand. I've known a few intelligent, resourceful women

16

who've fallen for useless, violent men, some who just couldn't get interested in any other type. I took two twenties and a ten out the change from the drinks and passed them to him. 'Don't drink it all, Barry. You need to rinse out that shirt and you could do with a deodorant and a mouthwash. See you tomorrow.'

He took the money and didn't speak. I watched him in the rear-vision mirror as I drove away. For a few seconds he wavered between turning left or crossing the street. Left took him to the corner and the pub. He squared his shoulders and crossed the street. There were signs that Barry White wasn't a completely spent force, but that didn't make me trust him one bit more.

I drove home to Glebe, stopping to buy some fish and some white wine on the way. I grew up on a diet of fried meat—chops, steak, sausages, bacon. That kind of tucker, plus large dollops of frustration, blocked my father's arteries and saw him off at a fairly early age, but I seem to have inherited my mother's constitution and temperament. She ate, drank and smoked what she liked, made it to seventy, and went complaining about her short innings. These days I exercise some dietary caution, but not with fish; the only way to cook it is the way my Uncle Jim said. He used to catch flathead, bream and tailor off Maroubra Beach after pulling up sandworms for bait with his fingers. 'Fry the fuckers!' was Uncle Jim's advice, and that's what I did.

I've lived alone since Glen Withers married

her policeman. I occasionally see a former girl-friend, Terry Kenneally, who came out of longish relationships more or less intact, like me. We have a meal together, go to a movie and sometimes to bed. There's nothing possessive about it. We're both looking for company and sex without complications. I can't say I prefer the arrangement to a passionate, committed relationship, but it's not too bad. I enjoy the gaps and solitary spells, knowing that they're not permanent.

I was in just such a spell at the moment with Terry, who was a tennis coach, away interstate with one of her hopefuls. Over the meal I lowered the level of the wine to halfway down the label and then quit, I made coffee and sat down to think about what I could be getting into with Barry White. It was hard to be optimistic. For years stories had circulated about cops with treasure troves—bales of marijuana, talcum powder tins full of cocaine, suitcases of money. As far as I knew none of these ships had ever come in, and the old rogue cops were all doing time or paying off their lawyer's bills by instalment. Still, White's story had a different ring and the man himself wasn't the standard sticky-fingered corrupt moron.

I took out a fresh notebook and started plotting my course through some of the hazards. First things first, and my priorities are not necessarily those of the person who's hired me. I had to check up on the reward. Were the terms and the accrued amount what White had stated? Along with that went a need to know more about Barry

White himself. Was my suspicion right that he'd done some time, and if so, for what? I needed to know the personnel of the police instigating team and, if possible, get some idea of their conclusions. Had laying charges been considered and, if so, against whom? That led to the obvious question that shapes any investigation—who benefits? White and I had talked about Ramona Beckett's victims as profiting from her death, but what about others—a lover, a family member? There was going to be some leg and telephone work involved as always and some favours to be asked for and maybe nothing to show at the end of it. But just maybe there'd be a good deal more to show than usual.

I watched the late-night news on television for a few minutes, long enough to tell that nothing had happened that hadn't been predicted in the morning or developed during the day. I turned on the radio to catch Phillip Adams' 'Late Night Live' program, but they were talking about the next millennium and I was happy just to wait for it. I played Paul Simon's *Graceland* through for the thousandth time and went to bed with Graham Richardson's autobiography which made me feel that the people I dealt with weren't so bad after all. My tennis gear was lying in a corner where I'd dropped it after my last game with Terry. I went to sleep thinking about her long brown thighs.

3

I never took to jogging, and riding a bicycle around Sydney these days is no fun, what with the foul air and the traffic. Like a lot of other people I've found that walking is the best exercise. You don't jar things, tend not to step in potholes and dog shit and you can think while you're doing it. I do a few kilometres in Glebe most mornings unless it's pissing down rain or I have to be somewhere early, and I try not to let that happen. It was March and cooler than it should have been after a summer that hadn't been up to much. I walked briskly through the park along with joggers, power-walkers, dog-walkers and others just walking.

When I moved to Glebe in the early seventies, you couldn't get down to the water below Jubilee Park. There were rows of old tin and fibro buildings in the way—a ship's chandler, a timber yard, an auto-electrician. That all got cleared away and the park was extended to the waterline with more trees and a paved walkway running all the way around to the canal. It was a 100 per cent improvement, and the upgrade is still going on to the west towards Johnston Street. More buildings have been cleared and the land detoxified. The plan is to let a section of it revert back to the wetland it once was. Good news for the birds. Normally, I go up the Crescent past the Lew Hoad Reserve to Bridge Road and make my way home that way, but since the work started on the Harold Park Paceway I've changed my route. They're extending the car park and building a stand out over Johnston's Creek. I don't approve. You used to be able to walk alongside the creek. It wasn't the flashest walk in the world, but at least it was public space. I wandered into the football ground and sat in the stands for a think.

A lot of birds sat there with me as if waiting for the wetlands to arrive. I was unsettled by some of the changes going on around here—the flight path, the Paceway, the development in Ross Street where a hectare or so of warehouses had come down, the Glebe Island Bridge for god's sake. I'd attended a meeting protesting the plan to build a marina on Blackwattle Bay and that was about as environmentally active as I'd been. I wondered, not for the first time, if I shouldn't think about moving. I didn't need a three-bedroom house with planes flying overhead, but I couldn't think of anywhere else I'd like to be except Bondi, and they were sure to start changing that soon.

I threaded my way through the streets and lanes that lead back to Bridge Road and the famil-iar sights and smells drove thoughts of moving out of my head. And no planes went over. I went home, showered and shaved and rang Frank

Parker, who I knew would be at his desk at ten past nine. Frank and I go back a long way. He married Hilde Stoner who was a tenant in this self-same house once, and they called their son after me. Frank's been pretty much put out to graze in administration, but every now and then he gets his hands dirty. We exchanged the usual male bullshit and I asked him what he knew about Barry White.

'A pity, that,' he said.

'How so?'

'He was the right sort of bloke for the job, or seemed to be. But the bastards at the 'Loo corrupted him. You'd have had to be a saint to resist some of the stuff that was on offer around there back then. Can I ask why you're interested?'

I'd have to give Frank some of the story to get what I wanted, but I wanted to intrigue him first. Frank Parker was a man with great curiosity. 'A job. He's got some information that could lead somewhere.'

'Oh, very helpful. Just ask me anything, I'll tell you everything I know.'

'Hang on a bit, Frank. Was he ever inside?'

'Let me think. Yeah, he did a very short stretch for conspiracy. I forget the details.'

'Leo Grogan?'

'Jesus, you're dipping deep in the bucket now. What is this, Cliff—a rollcall of crooked cops?'

'Was Grogan crooked?'

'You bloodhound, you. Not especially, as I remember. I worked with him for a while, if you could call what he did working. The man was drunk from morning to night. Just could not stand to have a dry throat. Come on, Cliff. I can't see the connection.'

'The connection is Ramona Beckett and a reward for information leading to blah, blah. Can you find out who was on the investigating team?'

'Sure.'

'I'd like to talk to him.'

'It's twenty years ago. He could be dead or in Noosa.'

'Seventeen years. I'll go to Noosa if I have to. If number one's dead I'll settle for number two or three. It's important, Frank.'

'Look, Cliff, we've taken on a sort of consultant to look into old unsolved cases when anything comes up. Name's Max Savage, good bloke.'

'Oh, yeah.'

'If I help you with this, can you bring him in?'

'I'd have to think about that.'

'He wouldn't want a bite of your reward. He's OK for money.'

'I don't know . . .'

'Sorry, Cliff. Them's the terms. I'll get you all the dope I can, if you'll play. But Max can get you more, much more. Added to that, I think you'd like him.'

I said nothing, intending the silence to be discouraging.

'Tell you what. See how you go for a day or two. I'll brief Max and he'll scratch around. If you decide to call him in I'll set up a meeting and I'll advise him from my high position in the force to give you every possible assistance.'

'You're a manipulative bastard.'

He laughed. 'You just got outmanipulated for once, that's all.'

The Cleveland is a boxing pub. The walls carry photos of old-time fighters and some not so old. Les Darcy and Jimmy Carruthers hold pride of place above the bar; Griffo's up there with Dave Sands and Vic Patrick and Tommy Burns and Jack Carroll. A couple of non-Australians get a grudging spot—Archie Moore, Freddie Dawson, Emile Griffith. The shrinking band of former fighters gathers there for reunions from time to time and they drink there regularly—not at 10 a.m. on a Tuesday though. There are two pool tables and couple of pinball machines but the pugs have been known to take steps if the players get too noisy when they're doing serious things like discussing whether Jack Carroll could've taken Benny Leonard or how Fenech would've gone against Famechon.

It's not what you'd call a dressy establishment. I wore drill trousers, a dark blue shirt and a cream linen jacket that has seen much better days. I'd eaten a ham sandwich and a couple of cold boiled potatoes before leaving home as blotter for the beer I'd be drinking. It's a trade that's hard on the liver. I spotted Barry White in a miasma of tobacco smoke at the end of the L-shaped bar. Just above where he sat, Ron Richards, who could beat anybody on his night, was glowering behind his

gloves. White raised his hand to me and then signalled the barman. *Fuck me*, I thought, *he's going
to buy me a drink.* Then I remembered that it was
my money. The middy was on the bar, sitting on
a much-used coaster, when I got there.

'Light? That right?' White said. He was on a
stool with two others drawn up near it.

I sat. 'That's right. Thanks. Cheers.'

'Yeah. Why'd you drink that piss?'

I took a long pull at the beer. 'Have you tasted
it lately? It's improved.'

He sighed. 'I suppose I'll be on it, or worse,
if I get on this health kick.'

'Don't worry, Barry. There's a way to go
before you reach that point.'

'True. Leo's late.'

'First hurdle.'

He drained his glass and pointed to it for the
barman's benefit. 'Don't say that and don't
worry—first drink of the day.' He stirred the pile
of change and the couple of five dollar notes on
the bar in front of him. 'See, I didn't drink the
lot.'

He was wearing the same clothes as yesterday
but his shirt looked fairly fresh and he didn't smell
as bad, although it was hard to tell with all the
tobacco fallout. Whoever the woman was who'd
lent him the money, she wasn't handy with a
needle. His jacket still lacked the button that
would enable it to be fastened smartly. The pub
was fairly quiet with just a few locals judiciously
wetting their whistles. Tuesday was two days
short of pension day and the beer money had to

be spun out. The Cleveland didn't go in for counter lunches or happy hours or any of the other attractions. It was a place for drinking and talking.

'So,' White said. 'You put out any feelers yet?'

'A few.'

'Frank Parker?'

'Let's just talk to Leo first.'

But he couldn't let it go. He sighed again as he fished out his Drum. 'He's a good cop, Parker.'

I was irritated and finished the middy quicker than I'd intended. 'He thinks the world of you, too.'

'You're a bastard, Hardy.'

'You said that before. Hello, this must be him or his twin brother.'

The man coming towards us could only have been a former cop. He had the walk, a sort of swagger that changes over the years as the belly gets bigger but still says, 'I can do things to you that you can't do to me.' He wasn't big, under six feet, but he was wide and thick through, especially around the middle. He wore a grey suit that had fitted him when he carried a few less kilos and a tie with some kind of emblem on it. Even in the gloom of the Cleveland, I could see that his nose was a mass of purple veins and a similar tracery spread across his cheeks.

'Yeah, that's Leo.' White signalled and a schooner of old appeared on the bar as Grogan reached us. He took it up and drank a third of it before dropping heavily onto a stool and shaking White's hand.

'G'day, Barry. Ta for the drink.' He pointed to White's diminished money pile. 'You're flush.'

'Temporarily in funds, Leo. D'you know Cliff Hardy?'

Grogan polished off another six or seven ounces. 'Heard of him. G'day, Hardy.'

'Leo.' I held up three fingers to the barman and took a closer look at Grogan's tie. The emblem was crossed boxing gloves. He saw me looking.

'State amateur light-heavy champ in 1966. You look as if you've gone a few rounds in your time.'

'Welter,' I said, 'Police Boys' Club stuff. Lost in the state semis to Clem Carter.'

The beers arrived, I paid and Grogan finished number one and took a surprisingly small sip of number two. The grog might have ruined his career and looks but perhaps he was still capable of shrewdness. 'I remember Carter. Good fighter but a dumb fucker.'

Clem had been a close mate of mine for a number of years. Grogan's assessment was harsh. Clem had escaped from gaol, taken me along for the ride at gunpoint to get even with the man who'd framed him and stolen his wife and ended up dead. 'He was unlucky,' I said. 'Like Barry here.'

Grogan snorted his amusement and took a solid pull on the schooner. 'Over to you, Barry. What the fuck're we all doing here, apart from remembering when we could throw a punch or two?'

White had fiddled with the cigarette he'd

rolled while Grogan and I had sparred. Now he lit it, drank some beer and pulled his stool in closer so that we were in a fairly tight ring. The paranoid thought suddenly occurred to me that this whole thing could be a set-up directed at me. I held a good store of secrets of one kind or another, and I knew there were people who could benefit from knowing things I knew. I studied the torsos of the two men closely, but they were both too flabby for me to tell whether there was any electrical equipment under their shirts. I resolved to say as little as possible until I could get a true sense of the meeting.

'A while back,' White said, 'you happened to tell me that you knew a thing or two about the Ramona Beckett case.'

Grogan sipped his beer and looked annoyed, but that might have been because he spilled some down his shirt. 'Oh, yeah. Did I?'

'You were . . . talkative. It rang a bell with me and I did a bit of checking. There was a reward out. There still *is* a reward.'

'Bullshit. Her father's dead.'

'It was in his fucking will, Leo. A quarter of a million bucks.'

Grogan looked at me. I shrugged and had to hope that concealed any surprise on my face. Barry White was the original corkscrew man. Here he was putting a twist on things right at the start. It made me wonder how many twists he'd introduced in his spiel to me.

'What do you reckon, Hardy?' Grogan said.

'It's one of the things I'm going to look into,' I said.

White puffed smoke away from our faces. 'You're our starting point, Leo. We can't make a move without your information. That's why you're in for twenty-five per cent.'

Grogan laughed. 'Jesus, I don't believe this. Well, at least I've got a drink out of it from youse. And I reckon I'll have another.' He drained the schooner and held it up without looking at the barman. For all his dismissiveness, he was watching Barry White closely. I was having trouble reading the signs in their behaviour towards one another. Animosity certainly, but also something else.

White didn't change expression. 'I didn't expect you to understand right off the bat. I know you've got no time for me, but this is serious. I've paid Hardy a five hundred dollar retainer and he's on two hundred a day and expenses—that's how serious it is.'

Grogan raised an eyebrow at me and I nodded. 'I didn't think you had a pot to piss in, Barry,' he said harshly. 'Didn't your missus take you for every fucking cent?'

'She did, the bitch. But I've got a backer.' White nodded as the barman looked inquiringly at the money pile. More drinks appeared and the pile shrunk to almost nothing. 'That's why I say your end is twenty-five per cent.'

Grogan started on his next drink. 'I wouldn't back you if you were the only horse in the race. When the pressure came on, you were ready to put every other bastard in to save your skin. Probably did just that.'

White shook his head. 'Ancient history, Leo. I've had my troubles just like you. Hardy did a short stretch for frigging around with evidence. We're none of us cleanskins, but this is a chance to get our hands on some real money.' He smiled and the old, booze-eroded charm was in his face. 'And to bring a criminal or criminals to justice.'

'Christ, you're a wanker,' Grogan said.

'Hardy doesn't think so. He's got the contacts, Leo. Frank Parker's a mate of his; he knows journos and lawyers. He can front the family. He knew the woman.'

'He's hardly said a fucking thing,' Grogan said.

'I bought you a drink.'

Grogan laughed. 'So you did. So you did. Fuck it, I'll play along. But I'll tell you something, Barry boy. If this comes to anything and you don't play straight with me, I'll see you get hurt.'

White butted his cigarette and reached for his fresh glass which he hadn't touched. 'Understood.'

'OK. This's what I know. Johnno Hawkins headed up the team that looked into the disappearance. I was in on it, but I was just a shit-kicker—driving, picking up the beer and pies and that. The case got a hell of a lot of publicity so Johnno was told to get busy and to come up with something quick. Well, he got busy all right, interviewed every bastard in sight and came up with sweet fuck-all.

'Things died down, the case went on the back

burner. One night I was out on the piss with this sheila I had then and Johnno and his wife, Peg. Did you ever meet her, Peggy Hawkins?'

White shook his head and drank. He was looking decidedly unhappy.

'Fucking good-looker,' Grogan said. 'Sharp features, skinny, but with tits out to here. They reckon she could ... never mind. Anyway, Johnno and Peg got into a fight, a real screaming match. This is back at their flat in Rose Bay. They were both pissed and I'd gone off with my tart for a root in one of the bedrooms. I reckon they'd forgotten about us. I heard Peg say to Johnno something like, "You wouldn't be able to afford her if you hadn't got all that money for keeping quiet about that ransom note." Johnno told her to shut up and he hit her. He resigned from the force soon after that and went up to the Gold Coast.'

White looked increasingly unhappy as Grogan's story unfolded. When it was finished he loosened his tie and slid the knot down. 'Johnno Hawkins is dead,' White said. 'Had a heart attack out fishing a year or so ago.'

Grogan took up his glass and raised it like a toast. 'That's right. But Peggy's still alive and fucking, last I heard.'

'Where?' I said. 'Still on the Gold Coast?'

'Yeah. She'll either be doing it for money or getting the money off the girls who're doing it for her.'

White smiled again and looked first at Grogan, then at me. 'We're away,' he said, as if he knew everything would come right in the end.

4

White pleaded with Grogan not to mention the matter to another living soul. Grogan sneered and agreed. He gave me his address and a telephone number where he could sometimes be reached, sank another schooner, and went off, not visibly excited.

'He's not a lot of laughs, is he?' I said to White.

'He's a shit. He wouldn't look pleased if his prick grew longer, but he'll play ball. Unlike me, he's got a pension, but he drinks most of it. Speaking of which . . .'

White's little stash had almost gone. I didn't want another drink but I ordered a round because we needed to talk some more.

'You started lying to Grogan right from the jump,' I said.

'I've played straight with you, that's all you need to worry about.'

'Maybe. He was threatening to kneecap you if you scammed him.'

'He's all piss and wind, always was. Sixty grand'll keep him sweet.'

I thought that was probably true, and it

seemed only fair that I should come out well ahead of Grogan for all the work I seemed likely to have to do. Suddenly, I realised that I was taking the thing seriously. I tried to pull back from that, but I couldn't help having the sort of feeling I had when I occasionally bought a lottery ticket—anticipation of a win is part of the pleasure and, most times, all of the pleasure. Still, I had to keep in mind that I was running a business.

'If I have to fly to the Gold Coast it'll cost a bit. How flush is this backer of yours?'

White looked doubtful. 'Haven't you got enough confidence in me yet to finance it yourself for a bit?'

'Perhaps. If Grogan's story is right, the question is, who was willing to shell out to suppress the note?'

White was fairly drunk, and it required an effort for him to assume a serious, investigative expression. 'That's right. A family member for sure. Didn't want her found. Bigger cut of the cake for him.'

'Or her. Do you know anything about Ramona's family set-up?'

'Shit, let me think. Like I say, I wasn't doing very much in there. A sister, maybe two sisters, and a brother. Might have been some half-brothers and sisters as well. Old Beckett had been married before.'

'Big help. What's in the will?'

'How the fuck would I know?'

'You know about the interest on the reward. Or is all that bullshit, too? I'm not getting any happier about paying my own way to the Gold Coast.'

'No, no, that's kosher about the reward. I got that from this accountant.'

'Go on.'

'Well, he's bent, you know. I got in touch with him over my fucking divorce settlement. Tried to get him to cook the books a bit in my favour. He would've, too, but Brenda's bloke was smarter. Anyway, he started talking about accountancy which I always reckoned must be the most boring fucking subject of the lot. Worse than . . . what was that crap I did at Uni? Torts, yeah, torts. Shit, that was dull.'

'Stick to the point, Barry, if you can.'

He pulled himself together again and I speculated on how many times he was capable of it in a day. 'This bloke had worked for the firm that handled the Beckett family finances. He told me the reward money was on the books. A million plus and counting. This was just a couple of days before I ran into Leo. Seren-fuckin'-dipity.'

The word brought me up short. It had been one of Glen Withers' favourites. It was partly the beer, partly keeping company with ex-policemen, partly who-knows-what, but I suddenly missed her terribly and the easy, comfortable time we had had together. Like some of the other women I'd loved and lost, she'd told me what was wrong with me when it came to the crunch—too change-able, too moody, too easily bored. I wasn't convinced. I always thought I was too soft on people, too ready to give the benefit of the doubt. I took another hard look at Barry White and saw the devious slackness under the charm, the mental sloppiness under the educated veneer. *Fuck him*, I thought. *If I can cut myself a bigger slice of this I will. But Barry White's not getting the benefit of any of my many doubts.*

I arranged to meet White again in two days time. I stipulated that as a kind of a test and he passed it. He wanted to ask me what I'd be doing and probably suggest other things, but he managed to prevent himself.

'By then I should know whether I'm up to flying to the Gold Coast or whether I'll just go to Bondi instead and forget the whole thing.'

'That sense of humour again. OK, Hardy. Spend my time well. I'll sniff around a bit myself, but don't worry, we won't cross wires.'

We skipped the handshake. I left the pub and stationed myself out of sight in a laneway. My car was a hundred metres away in a two-hour zone and the clock was ticking. About five minutes later, White emerged, brushing cigarette ash from his clothes. He cleared his throat and spat into the gutter. Then he took a comb out the top pocket of the blazer and ran it through his hair. Next came one of those pressurised gadgets that squirt breath-freshener into your mouth. He used it and spat again. He reached into his pants pocket and took out a slip of paper that could have been anything—a cheque, a dry cleaning receipt, a newspaper cutting. He looked at it and tucked it away with the comb. Then he prowled up and down the pavement impatiently, looking at his watch and staring at the nearest intersection. I headed for my car. You don't need to be Sherlock Holmes to tell when a man with a Cabcharge docket is waiting for a taxi.

I felt like a true professional jotting down the number of the cab as I waited behind it, two cars back, at the Abercrombie Street lights. Cabcharge dockets carry the name of the account on them and are carefully computer-processed. With a bit of luck, I should be able to find out who was paying for Barry's ride. We went up Cleveland Street and swung left beside the railway line. The taxi driver was fast and good, exploiting every gap he found, and it was tricky staying with him unobtrusively. Up Elizabeth Street past the golf shop, where at night the neon golfer hits neon balls into a neon hole, and a turn to the right up Wentworth Avenue. The taxi stopped beside the Connaught building and I caused irritation behind me by pulling in and waiting while Barry did his paperwork. He left the cab and I kerb-crawled after him. He was trying to fasten his jacket, forgetting that he was lacking the crucial button, as he went up the ramp, punched in a number on a keypad and entered the building. Interesting.

Harry Tickener runs his independent newspaper, *The Challenger*, out of an office in Surry Hills. The place smells of nothing but the very best coffee since Harry gave up chain-smoking Camels and drinking bourbon. Concerned about his figure,

Harry replaced his other habits with a devotion to coffee that might ream out his stomach lining in the end but will leave him a thin corpse. I hope it's a long time coming.

After the beer in the Cleveland it was good to sit over one of his massive flat whites and do exactly what Barry White had begged Leo Grogan *not* to do—talk openly to someone about the matter in hand. Harry's discretion is legendary; I've never known him to betray a confidence or to back away from naming the guilty men if he could possibly do it and stay out of gaol. We've given each other a hand in many ways over the years since he was a young, go-getting reporter and I was new in the private detective business. Once, not long after he took a golden handshake from the News Corporation and started up *The Challenger*, he asked me if I wanted a tag like 'with the assistance of Cliff Hardy' to appear with the journalist's by-line on a story I'd helped with. I used an obscenity and told him I'd sue if it happened.

'Ramona Beckett,' Harry said, propping his Nikes on the desk in front of him and wrapping his pale, freckled hands around a coffee mug. 'Sure, I remember. I was still at *The News* then, protecting incompetent arses. Didn't work on it myself.'

'Were there any whispers?'

'Like what?'

'Barry White has suggested that perhaps not all the cops were playing with straight bats.'

'You shock me. Dealing with Barry White. No,

not that I remember. Wasn't she some kind of blackmailer?'

'Allegedly. Yes, she was.'

Harry shrugged. 'How hard would anyone try to find her then?'

'Don't forget the reward. I'd like to know what was in her dad's will.'

'Would you now? Well, it would've been filed for probate. You'd have your ways of getting a squiz at that, wouldn't you, son?'

'Yeah, I'll take a look, but I'd also like to talk to the lawyer, get the flavour of the thing as it were. That's why I'm here taking up your time. I thought that if you were to ask nicely, that librarian in at *The News* who used to fancy you would probably look up the cuttings and get the lawyer's name.'

'Seventeen years. Chances are he's dead.'

'You're not, I'm not.'

'True, surprisingly.' Harry punched buttons on a phone. I drank some more coffee and got, or thought I got, a lift from it. I wandered around the suite of small offices. *The Challenger* does well and is always threatening to grow. When this happens, Harry does what he calls a 'pruning'. He wants it to stay on a scale he can control. Also he hates sacking people, so he keeps the staff at the same size. Their loyalty is fierce. I knew all of them slightly and exchanged a few words as I made my tour. Maddy Allbright, Harry's chief assistant, was chuckling over a piece of copy.

'What?' I said.

'Here's a six-foot four-inch lesbian who wants

to be a priest. She claims she's being discriminated against on grounds of sex, sexuality and height.'

'That's a tall order.'

'Go away.'

Harry waved at me. 'Got it,' he said. 'It seems old Beckett married a younger woman and he took her lawyer on. Not a wise move to my mind, but there you are. Name's Wallace Cavendish. I've written it all out on a Post-it so you can stick it somewhere.'

I put the mug on the desk where the ring it would make would join a thousand others. 'Thanks, Harry.'

'I also asked Marjorie for copies of the main cuts on the Beckett case. I'll fax them to you if you like.'

'Forever in your debt. I must make sure there's some paper in the machine. It's all been a bit slow lately.'

'If you turn up anything interesting . . .'

'It goes without saying,' I said.

I walked out into the early-afternoon sunshine, completely sober, my mood much improved by the meeting with Harry, but very hungry. My first stop was a sandwich bar much patronised by Harry's people, where they build elegant structures that somehow hold together and don't drip on you. I ate the sandwich sitting on a bench in one of the little paved squares that have been carved out in the middle of the residential and industrial busyness. I shared the space but not the sandwich with some disappointed pigeons and seagulls. The weather had improved as the day went on and, professionally, the outlook wasn't too bad either. I had a police consultant to consult, a lawyer to meet, newspaper cuttings to read and a widow to visit at the Gold Coast. I've had much worse starts.

5

I drove the short hop to Darlinghurst, parked in my usual spot, and headed for my office. The way Harry Tickener worked, the faxed cuttings could be spewing out of the machine right now. The area around St Peters Lane has changed a hell of a lot since I first lobbed there, but the change seems to have stalled, which suits me. I used to like the accretion of posters on the walls—rock gigs, religious meetings, political rallies—dating back years. The bill posters tended not to overlay them exactly, or they peeled off and you could trace history on the walls the way archaeologists read stratified deposits. Nowadays, the council employs someone to strip them off. Sad.

I went up the stairs humming some Sinatra song or other and was embarrassed when I saw a man waiting outside my door. I'm not a tuneful hummer, as several women have told me. At least I have the sense not to sing. The man looked unthreatening—late middle-aged or more, stocky with thinning grey hair, a slightly rumpled light-weight suit to match, briefcase. Still, nothing to say there wasn't a pair of brass knucks in the

41

briefcase at his feet. I slowed down to give him time to make the first move. Someone pretending to be passive, but intending to be active, sometimes betrays the intention by body language. Sometimes. This guy was harmless stillness itself.

'Mr Hardy?' he said loudly, taking a step away from the wall and leaving the briefcase where it was.

I stopped humming. 'That's right.'

He stuck out a surprisingly big, meaty paw. 'Glad to meet you. I'm Max Savage.'

The name registered—Frank Parker's consultant—but this was all very disconcertingly premature. I shook the hand and dug for my keys. 'You've jumped the gun,' I muttered.

'What was that?'

The volume of his voice forced me to look at him. 'I said you've jumped the gun.'

He nodded. 'Jumped the gun, that's right. I'm afraid I have. I'll explain when we get inside.'

The light wasn't good in the corridor, a matter of dirty windows and low wattage in the bulbs, which was why I hadn't noticed the small hearing aids in both ears. I unlocked the door and ushered him in. He bent easily to pick up the briefcase and stepped smartly past me. For a mature-age citizen he moved pretty smoothly. The office has a tiny vestibule, about big enough to hold a bicycle, and then the room itself. Max Savage went in, put his briefcase down and stood by the client chair. I had the odd feeling that he was directing the traffic, willing me to get behind the desk to my allotted place. Instead I went over to the fax machine and examined the long roll of paper that had come through. Good old Harry.

I looked straight at him. 'Sit down, Mr Savage,' I said.

'Thank you.' He sat, and the contrast with the last man who'd sat there couldn't have been more extreme. Whereas Barry White had been a mass of tics and fidgets and habitual gestures, Savage was a model of harmony and control. He waited for me to sit down and looked as if it wouldn't worry him if he had to wait an hour or so. I tore off the fax paper and let the roll settle. Then I sat down.

'I don't want to be rude, but Frank Parker was going to give me some time to get back to him,' I said. 'This is all a bit premature, isn't it?'

'It is and I'm sorry. But as you can imagine, the telephone is a difficult instrument for me. I have to use a relay service or get someone to interpret, as it were, for me. That's cumbersome and people tend not to want to go through the rigmarole. I find face-to-face meetings much more productive. As to the rush, I'll be frank with you, Mr Hardy. The police service takes a dim view of me on the whole. Frank is one of my few supporters. I've had bugger-all to do since I was approached and this is the first chance for me to get my teeth into something. I'm excited by it. So, as you say, I jumped the gun.'

I realised that I liked him. He was direct and honest, not common characteristics in the people I meet, and he seemed to treat his disability matter-of-factly, so that I felt comfortable with it.

Still, you have to know exactly who you're dealing with.

'How deaf are you?' I asked.

'Very, but not totally. I get a fair bit in on some frequencies and next to nothing on others. In a quiet setting like this I can hear your voice more or less. You speak very clearly. Of course, I don't really need to hear it.'

'How's that?'

'I'm a very good lip-reader. You open your mouth when you speak and you haven't got any facial hair so I can pick up what you're saying pretty exactly. Then there's the body language.'

I was interested. 'Body language?'

'Yep. People express themselves in the way they move as much as in what they say. A lot of what's said is superfluous anyway—repetitive, retracted, ambiguous. I can tell if someone's speaking positively, negatively or speculatively from the way they move their bodies and their facial expressions. Then, with the bit of hearing and the lip-reading I don't miss much.'

'Must be fun in a bus.'

'It can be. I've picked up things that'd make your hair curl.'

'OK. But this *is* all a bit previous. I'm still scratching around with this thing and . . .'

'Let's scratch together. I've learned a thing or two that could be useful.'

I glanced across at the faxes and he raised an eyebrow. It was then I noticed a mark on the side of his face, like a birthmark but somehow different. It was slightly shiny and I suspected that he had applied some kind of make-up to it. His face was lean and firm, his dark eyes were deep-set and steady. No spectacles, faint frown lines suggesting contacts had replaced them.

'Newspaper cuttings on the Beckett matter,' I said. 'From a friend.'

Savage nodded. 'Harry Tickener. Parker speaks well of him. I'd like to see them.'

It amused me to think about what my client would say if he could see me now, chatting away and perhaps about to share confidences with this grey-hair. One thing I knew, I put more trust in Max Savage than in Barry White. But I was at a disadvantage; Frank Parker had evidently told Savage something about me, whereas I knew nothing about him. I leaned back in the chair. 'Tell me a bit about yourself, Mr Savage. How did you lose your hearing?'

Savage smiled, showing strong, even teeth that helped to give his face structure. 'I was a cop, what else? I was on the South Australian force for more than twenty years. Made acting Inspector. Didn't like it much, all bloody paperwork. I went out with the detectives one night to pull in one of these ram-raid bastards. To make a long story short, I wound up at close quarters with him and a sawn-off shottie up against a wall. Gun went off and killed him.' He raised a hand to his face. 'I got burns and a bit of blast, but the worst thing was it buggered up my hearing.'

'Bad luck,' I said. 'So you got invalided out?'

He smiled again. 'Not right away. The hearing loss was sort of gradual but I could tell it was going. I got a doctor to pass me for a year or two and I took the promotion. I learned to lip-read and I got these miniature hearing aids, but they spotted me in the end and saw me off.'

'So how did you get this job?'

'Partly contacts. I worked with New South boys on quite a few occasions, but mostly because no-one else wanted it. What did Frank tell you?'

'Next to nothing.'

'It's all bullshit on the face of it. The title's just window-dressing. The empire-builders don't actually want me to do anything, but they can point to me if they get asked what's being done about these open cases. A few people, like Frank, think I can really be useful. I think so, too. I intend to be useful and I expect I'll have to be a nuisance to do it.'

I liked that. 'Nuisance value' is a good expression in my book, and I had a feeling that Mr Savage was going to display plenty of it. The opposition would be formidable, though. 'You're going to be unpopular,' I said. 'Have you got a family or . . .'

It was apparent that he was picking up every word I said, and I was deliberately speaking quietly. He shook his head and leaned forward intently. His fists, resting on his knees, clenched hard. He'd been speaking in a normal tone but now the volume went up a bit. 'No. My wife died a few years back. No kids. I'm on good, indexed super from the South Australian department. Look, Mr Hardy . . .'

I grinned at him. 'Cliff, Max.'

He cleared his throat, eased back in the chair and his hands relaxed. 'Good. Cliff. Right. I know you've got a living to make and people to protect . . .'

'Call it keep sweet, at least for a while.'

'I don't want to get in the way of any of that and I won't if I can help it. But this Ramona Beckett case is bloody interesting and anyone with any kind of a feel for detective work would like to sort it out.'

'True. And from the angle I'm coming at there's a hell of a lot of money involved.'

'But you wouldn't frame anyone or misrepresent things to get it?'

'No.'

'We can work together, don't you reckon?'

'Mm. I'm a bit worried about you and the cop culture, I must admit. I was expecting you to be an academic or a computer genius or something. As things stand now, a former policeman involved looks pretty dirty.'

'Johnno Hawkins? That's not a problem. I've got no time for blokes like him. Never did.'

'Why d'you mention Hawkins?'

'I've been reading the files, Cliff. If Hawkins was fair dinkum about that investigation I'll shout you drinks for a month.'

There didn't seem to be any point in pussy-footing around. I told Max pretty well everything I knew. He made notes while I talked and only asked the odd question, mostly about White and Grogan. When I finished I scissored the fax, ran the sheets through the photocopier and handed

47

the copies to him. He thanked me, folded them and put them away in his briefcase. 'Make interesting reading. OK, what do you want to ask me?'

'I'd like to see all the investigation reports.'

Max held his hand a metre above the floor. 'The file's about this thick.'

'Shit. Hawkins' notebook, then.'

'Notebooks. He filled half a dozen at least. Mostly bullshit, wool to pull over eyes. What would you be looking for specifically?'

'Obviously, trying to get a line on who would've paid him to run dead.'

'Right, well he interviewed everyone of course. Some of them a couple of times. You think you'd be able to smell the phoney one?'

'Or ones. Who knows how many of them were in on it, if it happened.'

'I'll dig out the notebooks and we can go through them together. There's one thing that worries me. Say it all happened the way your informant suggests, the likelihood is someone else was in on it, someone higher up, giving Hawkins protection. That person might still be around and might have a lot to lose.'

I hadn't thought of that. Dealing with disgraced and retired cops is one thing, dealing with cops still in place and powerful is quite another. After my recent de-licensing and reinstatement I was vulnerable in a way I hadn't been before. And, as a good number of people found out in the seventies and eighties, a disgruntled policeman is a danger to life and limb.

'How sealed-off can you keep your inquiries?' I asked.

'Not very. I've already done the obvious thing—called for all sorts of files to provide a haystack for the needle. But if anyone gets really interested ...' He opened his hands expressively.

'Yeah,' I said. 'But that cuts both ways. If *you* get to hear of anyone taking an interest, that could be a bird flushed.'

Max smiled. 'I like your devious mind. How do you see it from here? Oh, shit, I'm assuming ...'

'You can,' I said. 'I think it'll be intriguing, as you say.'

'Yes, yes, for sure. OK, the notebooks, then ...'

'It'd be good if you could pull Barry White's file and see if there's any hint on who his benefactor might be.'

Max made a note. 'Right, and see if Hawkins had any particularly useful mates. What are you going to do?'

'Talk to the lawyer if I can. See if the reward story's kosher. If it is, I'll need to talk to the widow up on the Gold Coast. The trouble with this thing is, even if we get a line on who paid off Hawkins to suppress the note, it doesn't tell us anything about who killed Ramona Beckett. Not necessarily.'

'I see what you mean,' Max said. 'Against that, there's a chance the guilty party went all the way with the kidnappers.'

'Maybe.'

'I might come to Queensland with you, if that's OK. I'm on expenses. I wouldn't mind meeting a widow.'

'We've got two widows here. Don't forget Mrs Beckett.'

'One'd be enough,' Max said.

6

After an exchange of phone numbers we agreed to a meeting, same time, same place, in two days. I read through the newspaper cuttings that carried headlines like 'HEIRESS DISAPPEARS', 'MILLION-AIRE'S DAUGHTER VANISHES' and 'SOCIETY BEAUTY FEARED DEAD'. The photographs brought back sharp memories. Ramona Beckett had not exactly been beautiful—all her edges and lines were too sharp and defined for that. There was nothing comfortable and soothing about her the way there is with truly beautiful women, but she had something extra that more than compensated for this deficiency. Sexy wasn't quite the word for her either. You wanted to touch and you wanted her to touch you is the best way of putting it, and when those dark eyes swung your way, you had the feeling that it might be possible.

I could remember our social meetings and our one and only sexual encounter quite vividly, although a lot of alcohol was consumed each time. She was well read and very bright, also funny in a caustic way. On the night that I put the screws on her, we went to her flat in Potts Point

51

after dinner at the Bourbon and Beefsteak, her favourite hangout. We were clawing at each other on the stairs. If she was acting I didn't care. I wanted to touch every inch of her and enter her wherever she'd let me. She was wearing a black dress, cut low in the front and back, with thin straps and a short, floating skirt. A black ribbon choker with a pearl set in it emphasised the slenderness of her long neck. Her dark hair fell to her square shoulders and smelled of flowers and tobacco. We were both smokers and our breaths must have been foul with alcohol and Chesterfields, but in those days no-one cared. I could almost span her waist with my hands and her long, thin legs, dark stockings and high heels were sexual signals all saying 'Go!'

I got an erection, sitting there at the desk thinking about it, and got up to break the spell. I tried to remember how I'd felt when the story about her disappearance broke in the papers. All the information, such as it was, was there in front of me in the faxes: she was seen in a restaurant in Manly on a quiet Monday night, dining alone. Her car, a white Celica coupé, was found garaged under her apartment block. How she got to Manly, why she hadn't driven, hadn't been determined. She left the restaurant alone and was seen walking towards the ferry and that was about it. The reports that followed were mostly about the lack of progress in the police investigation. There were speculative stories about Ramona's political ambitions and very veiled hints about her methods. Her 'friendships' with 'prominent political figures' were mentioned, but nothing specific, no names.

As I flicked through the sheets the initial reactions came back to me. I had been deeply puzzled that a person with so much intelligence and energy had taken such a bad turning. I had wondered what had made her the driven, ruthless creature she was and had no idea of the reason. We had mostly talked money and politics. Another reaction came back as well, something that had surprised me at the time—I remember laughing hard at some of the things she'd said, admiring the shrewdness of other observation. Then there was the intensity of the brief sexual transport: I thought then and still did—what a waste of an exceptional human being!

The cuttings reminded me that Joshua Beckett had made his initial millions from digging up bits of Australia and selling it overseas. Then he invested in fast food outlets, shopping malls, medical centres and pharmaceutical companies. It sounded as if he had the knack of turning one dollar into a hundred, a hundred into a thousand and so on. His first wife had divorced him early in his career but the custody of their son and daughter was shared. The son, Sean, was thirty-six at the time of Ramona's disappearance and held an executive job in one of Dad's businesses. The daughter, Estelle, was said to be 'developing her own fashion label'.

There was nothing much on record about the first Mrs Beckett and the reason wasn't hard to see. Ramona's beautiful mother, Gabriella, née Vargas, had supplied the genes that shaped Ramona. She was a tall, slender woman with hawklike features and a wide slash of a mouth. At forty-plus when her daughter disappeared, she was twenty years younger than her husband. All news reports described her as 'distraught', although in the photos I saw I would call her 'composed'. She was the daughter of Tomas Luis Vargas who had been the Spanish Ambassador to Australia in the 1950s, so maybe she had learned a bit about composure.

The story made a big splash in the Sydney papers, especially the tabloids, and even ran for a while in the national press, but it faded when nothing new turned up. It got new legs when the reward was announced but, again, no results, no staying power. Other bad news crowded Ramona off the front and inside pages—Prince Charles visited for the funeral of 'Pig Iron' Bob, three Amanda Marga members were arrested for the Hilton bombing and an aircraft hit a house in Melbourne, killing six members of a family.

I read the cuttings through a couple of times, taking note of the names and trying to build up a picture of the players and their actions. The Beckett family hardly figured, other than photographically. No statement of any interest was reported from any one of them. Detective Sergeant John Hawkins was prominent early. He had the looks for the job—dark, cropped hair, hollow cheeks, immaculate three-piece suit. I have an instinctive distrust of any man who'd wear a three-piece suit in Sydney, especially in January and February. Early on, Johnno made all the right noises about 'our investigations are proceeding satisfactorily' and 'we have several promising leads to follow', then there was a slide to 'we are calling on members of the public to assist' and down to 'information is being sifted'. In the end it looked as if he bored the journalists to death, but that impression may have been prejudiced by the line I was following.

Over the years that followed there had been several follow-up stories and the Beckett case had even made its way into the 'historical' section of one Sunday tabloid, like the Burns–Johnson fight, the Japanese mini-submarines in Sydney Harbour and the disappearance of the Beaumont children. No new data emerged and, reading between the lines, it was clear that Gabriella Beckett had turned away any reporters who had approached her.

I smoothed out the faxes and folded them so that Ramona Beckett, in the classic picture—the one that all the papers ran and was featured over the following years when the story was dusted off and dragged out again—looked up at me. Her forehead was high, but not too high, her nose was hooked but nicely so, her mouth was like her mother's—a wide, thin-lipped gash, promising sin. The heavy, hooded eyes seemed to stare and probe into me and I had the strange feeling that she would try to get even with me from beyond the grave. *Bullshit*, I thought. I put the faxes in a folder and closed the cover on the staring eyes.

When a will is probated, the mechanism is an application to the state Supreme Court from the executor for the go-ahead to put the deceased's wishes into practice. The document and some supporting affidavits have to be lodged and, after the court grants the request, the whole lot is available for scrutiny by beneficiaries and other interested parties. Strictly speaking, I shouldn't be allowed to look at the documents, but like most PEAs I had an understanding with a deputy registrar who was willing to stretch the definition of 'interested party' as long as it didn't get him in trouble. I rang him and got the reference number which would enable me to avoid the long wait to look at the microfiche register on Level 5 of the Supreme Court building. He'd give me a pass to Level 6 where the wills are filed.

Next I had to locate Harry Tickener's Post-it. I found it stuck to a leaf of my notebook and telephoned the Martin Place office of Wallace Cavendish, solicitor to the Beckett family. I stated my business in guarded, almost cryptic terms to a secretary with an extraordinarily appealing voice, and was told that the man himself was away interstate.

'Due back when?' I asked.

'Tonight.'

'I'd like to see him tomorrow.'

'That may not be possible,' said honey-voice. 'If I may have your number I'll advise you when Mr Cavendish will be free.'

And that was the best I could do. I drove down William Street and parked in College Street at one of the meters that had become free as the earliest of the commuters on flexi-time started to move out. I walked through Hyde Park and St James' Park to the Supreme Court. Level 5 is always busy with bonds, bail and other matters being settled. It was a relief to get the nod from my contact and bypass the people clutching their tickets and waiting for their numbers to show up in big red figures. Things are quieter on Level 6. I paid over the ten dollars necessary to get a copy of a will probated between 1850 and 1986. The public can get a look at any will but only an executor can see the full list of assets and their disposal. For the purpose of this exercise, and for a price, I was an executor. After a fairly short wait the documents were produced. A probated will can be a file as slim as a magazine insert or a hefty document. Joshua Beckett's was somewhere in between. I flicked through it as I rode down in the lift.

The bulk of the estate, which was valued at 6.8 million dollars, went to Beckett's wife. There was a bequest of seven hundred and fifty thousand dollars to Sean Ian Beckett and sizeable shares in several companies. Estelle Lucy Beckett got half a million dollars and some smaller stock packages. A few charities came in for a whack and a couple of people who sounded like long-term domestic servants also did OK. No mention of the first Mrs B. The sum of two hundred and fifty thousand dollars was invested in a portfolio to be jointly administered by James Hills of Hills and Associates, accountants, and Wallace Cavendish, solicitor. The funds were at all times to be available at call, and Cavendish and Mrs Beckett jointly were authorised to dispense them to any person or persons 'whose information leads to the conviction of those responsible for the death of my dear daughter, Ramona Louise Beckett'. Good on you, Josh.

7

Mrs Horsfield, Wallace Cavendish's secretary, was a dumpy, homely woman with a beautiful voice. She'd phoned me at 8 a.m. to say that her lord and master could see me at ten. Meaning she'd communicated with Cavendish some time late yesterday and he'd agreed to a meeting virtually as early as it could be set up. That was interesting. I wore my best, that is to say my only suit—a dark blue lightweight double-breaster that hadn't gone out of fashion, although the lapels were possibly not quite exactly the right shape for this year. Mrs Horsfield seemed to approve of my appearance. She'd probably been expecting a leather-jacketed thug, which I would have easily provided in a different context.

'Just one minute, Mr Hardy,' she said in a voice that would have lured most sailors onto the rocks, except that her second chin wobbled. 'Please take a seat. Mr Cavendish is dealing with a tiny detail, then he'll be with you.'

I nodded and sat down in a deep leather-covered chair that seemed to swallow me up. The magazines on the table beside me catered for just about all tastes—*Golf Today*, *Tennis Australia*, *Australian Business*, *Australian Bride*, *Home and Garden*, *Best Investments Guide*. I leafed through the tennis magazine sceptically, wondering what effect it would have had on Rod Laver if he'd been called the new Lew Hoad at nineteen, the way they were calling Mark Phillipousos the new Pancho Gonzales. Darren Cahill had been the new Roy Emerson; Patrick Rafter the new John Newcombe . . .

'Mr Cavendish will see you now, Mr Hardy.'

She showed me into an office not quite as big as a tennis court. The walls were book-lined but leaving plenty of room for paintings, framed degrees and awards of one sort or another. You could do at least four different things in that room—work at the big teak desk, hold a conference at the big table, have a chat and coffee around a low table or have a sleep on the wide sofa. I assumed that there was a bar somewhere, so make that five things; if there was a TV, six. The blinds were set to allow in enough morning light to read by but not too much. The air-conditioning, keeping the room at a comfortable temperature, was a faint whisper in the background.

Cavendish stood up behind his desk as I came in. He was taller than me, getting on for 190 centimetres, and he looked fit in his blue shirt, dark trousers and red tie with braces to match. The braces were a jaunty touch in an otherwise very serious-looking man. He was somewhere between fifty and sixty, impossible to be precise because his smooth skin had a slightly artificial look as if he'd had a facelift, but that could have just been good genes and good dietary habits. His hair was thick, worn long and with plenty of grey in it. I'd have been willing to bet that his teeth were good and his prostate likewise. He took off horn-rimmed reading glasses as I moved across the room and I could see what a good prop they'd be in meetings when making a play with those deep-set but large grey eyes— put 'em on for something serious, whip 'em off when going for a laugh.

'Mr Hardy.' His handshake was firm, his accent what used to be called 'educated Australian'.

'Mr Cavendish, thank you for seeing me.'

'Sit down, sit down. I can't give you very long, but I must admit I was intrigued by what you told Mrs Horsfield.'

I unbuttoned my jacket and sat down, wishing I had some red braces to show. 'I think I can be a little more frank with you. My client has information that may throw light on Ramona Beckett's disappearance.'

Cavendish nodded. 'So I gather. This is very late in the day. May I know the name of your client?'

'No.'

'Well . . .'

'I'd like to ask you some questions.'

'Go ahead. I'll try to be more forthcoming than you.'

'Is the reward of two hundred and fifty thousand dollars still on offer?'

He hesitated and I watched him closely. *Would he tell the truth, the whole truth and nothing but the truth?* He didn't. 'Yes,' he said. 'It is.'

Not quite a lie, but an interesting understatement to say the least. 'Can you tell me whose idea it was to post the reward?'

He picked up his glasses and fiddled with the arms, bringing them together and separating them, as if one was the 'no comment' arm and the other was 'the name'.

The left arm was folded in. 'I believe Mr Beckett conceived the idea.'

'Did the other members of the family approve?'

The position of the arms reversed. 'I really couldn't comment on that. I can't quite see where your questions are leading. Perhaps you could be more specific about this information.'

Fair enough. And I couldn't see any harm in stirring the possum. 'Only a little,' I said. 'It seems to suggest the involvement of a member of the family in the . . . disappearance.'

'That's preposterous!'

I had a feeling that I didn't have much more of his expensive time and there was no point in fencing with him. He was smart, experienced and looked utterly secure. It was time for the broadsword. 'She was a blackmailer, Mr Cavendish. I know because I frustrated one of her scams. She must have been an embarrassment to the family, perhaps even a threat. Maybe she went too far . . .'

'That is ridiculous. Absurd. If you go about saying these things . . .'

'She's officially dead. Anyone can say what they like about her.'

'I mean . . . implying that Gabriella or . . .'

The first slip and my tactic was not to notice it. I dropped my eyes, took out my notebook and made a play of checking a few things off. Cavendish glanced at his watch. Then I tried for my most winning smile, flipped the notebook closed and tucked it and the pen away in the inside pocket of my suit coat. All that took a second or two. 'I know you're busy. So am I. Like me, you must have a lot of things on your plate. Did you know Cy Sackville, by the way?'

Cy was my lawyer and my friend. He'd been shot to death about a year ago and I missed him badly. But Cy would understand if I used the connection. Hell, he'd have been amused.

'Yes, indeed. A fine man. A tragedy.'

'Right. I killed the guy who killed him.'

'Ah. Yes, I believe I . . .'

'To be honest with you, Mr Cavendish, I don't know how far I'm going to go with this. What I've got, it's all a bit thin.'

I was counting on Cavendish wanting to get me out of the hair of his no doubt very financially useful clients as quickly as possible. He dropped the glasses onto the desk. 'Yes?'

'I'd like to see Mrs Beckett. I reckon I can manage to get to the son and daughter on my own, but the widow could be a problem. You could

63

arrange it and be present. A quick meeting, a few questions, that's all. What do you say?'

This was more than he'd bargained for and he took some time over it. His high brow furrowed and I decided he was closer to sixty than fifty. Worry tends to work against a superficial youthfulness. 'What,' he said slowly, 'would the nature of the questions be?'

I shrugged. 'It's been a long time. Perhaps certain things have changed. For one thing, I'd like to ask Mrs Beckett if she knows of any propositions that were put to certain policemen.'

'What propositions?'

I shook my head. 'Depending on her answer, I'd like to ask her about her relations with her stepchildren.'

'I can tell you that. They are distant.'

'I'd like to hear it from her.'

'I don't know.' He glanced at his watch again.

'You seem very protective,' I said.

'With reason. Mrs Beckett is not a young woman.'

I nodded. 'About the same age as yourself, I'd guess.'

He let that pass although he didn't like it. 'As you must have gathered, I'm a friend to Mrs Beckett as well as a legal adviser. She leads a life of some seclusion and you would find considerable difficulty in getting to see her. A great many journalists have tried over the years and failed.'

'I know that,' I said. 'But when you tell her what I've told you, she may feel differently.'

'You've told me almost nothing, but I take

your point.' He stood up, indicating closure, and to give himself the height advantage. 'I'll be in touch with you, Mr Hardy. I assume Mrs Horsfield has the number?'

I stayed in my seat, denying him the advantage and hoping to make him feel just a little abrupt and foolish. 'Mrs Horsfield has a beautiful voice,' I said.

He looked surprised, thought about sitting down again, decided against it, rested his hands uncomfortably on the desk in front of him. 'Yes, she does indeed. She was an opera singer. A contralto. Do you like opera, Mr Hardy?'

That was the opening I'd been waiting for— the chance for the broadsword thrust. I stood up quickly and buttoned my jacket. 'I despise it,' I said. 'Silly stories, boring music and lousy acting. I hope you don't waste too much money on it. I look forward to hearing from you soon, Mr Cavendish.'

I made the route march to the door, feeling Cavendish's shrewd grey eyes boring into my back. That never hurt anyone. I flashed a smile at the contralto and took the stairs instead of the lift. *Muy macho.*

I'd parked near my office and walked down to Martin Place. As I strolled back I was feeling pretty pleased with myself. It's not every day you put a high-priced lawyer on the back foot and maybe, just maybe, get to go where fearless journalists have failed to tread. Cavendish's unwillingness to be fully frank about the reward, his relationship with the widow, and his remark about the 'distance' between her and her stepchildren interested me. I pondered these things as I walked up William Street, keeping my breathing as shallow as possible—the less of that sort of air you take in the better.

There was no-one in the corridor this time and not much action in the building as a whole. The other commercial tenants—a desk-top publisher of pornography, a mail-order coin and stamp merchant, an acupuncturist and a South African whose business I'm not sure of—tend to be late arrivers. The few residential occupants on the floor below me, where renovations happened, but petered out, sleep late. I went into the gloomy office and saw the message light blinking on the answering machine. I hit the button as I shrugged out of my suit coat. Two callers. The first was from the bank telling me that a cheque I'd been having some trouble with had finally been re-presented and cleared. The caller gave the time as 11.39. Just ten minutes back. The machine played the next message. Barry White's agitated voice, sober and high-pitched, cut through my complacent mood like a chainsaw through pine.

'Hardy! Hardy! Where the fuck are you? I'm in trouble. Jesus Christ! Get here. Rose Street. Quick as you can.'

8

The boarding house looked peaceful enough. A couple of residents lounged at the gate yarning to anyone who would stop. They stepped aside to let me pass and went on talking as if I didn't exist. I went up the steps and in the front door to the familiar smells neglected and neglectful men generate—a compound of sweat, tobacco, beer, fast food, urine and dirty socks. There were two occupied rooms on the ground floor along with a kitchen and a sitting room, and I guessed three or four on the two levels above. That put Barry White's room, number 4, one floor up.

I don't know where White had lived when he was riding high as a corrupt copper, but it must have been a million times better than this. The stairs were narrow and dark with gaps in the uprights and a rickety railing. The carpet was worn and lifting, a hazard to anyone with poor eyesight or a load on board, and that most likely applied to many of the residents. I went up quickly and reached a landing dimly illuminated by a small window that hadn't been cleaned since the end of World War I. I knocked on number 4;

I got no answer but the door swung slightly inwards.

I went in and at first noticed only that the room smelled cleaner than the hall and the stairs. My eyes had adjusted to the poor light and the brightness in here made me blink. White's room must have been one of the better ones in the establishment. He had, as well as the room itself, a glassed-in balcony, and light was flooding in from there through closed French windows with clean panes. White had made an effort. The bed was neat; some books and magazines were neatly stacked on a dresser beside it. On a small table there was a toaster, a loaf of bread and a tub of margarine. A carton of long-life milk, a packet of tea and one of sugar and a jar of instant coffee were lined up precisely on a shelf.

I opened the French windows and saw my client. He was sitting in a cane chair and he was wearing the same shirt and tie I'd seen him in on the previous two days. The only difference was that the tie and the front of the shirt were stained dark brown with his blood. His head had flopped forward towards his chest but hung there, as if he might lift it at any minute. But he wouldn't. I didn't need to feel for a pulse or put a mirror to his mouth. The blood was in a pool in his lap below his paunch and had soaked down the length of both trouser legs. When you lose that much blood you're history.

I let out the breath I'd been holding and took a look around the balcony. There was almost nothing to see. Lino on the floor, a couple of struggling plants in pots on a shelf and a packet of Drum and a lighter with an ashtray on the floor. Three butts. The windows were fixed except for a small louvred section which stood partly open. This was evidently where Barry sat when he smoked, thought his thoughts and dreamed his dreams. He didn't have to worry about giving up the grog and the smokes and losing weight and eating lettuce now. A slight breeze came in through the window and ruffled his freshly trimmed hair.

On closer examination it was clear that White had been shot twice at close range. One of the bullets must have hit an artery that pumped out the blood. Perhaps the second shot came later, as insurance. It had taken me about forty minutes to get to the boarding house and White must have made his call after 11.39 from a phone box nearby or somewhere in the house. He couldn't have been dead for more than about half an hour before I got there. There was no smell of cordite in the air but with modern weapons there isn't necessarily. And a silencer can take care of the noise. The police could question the residents about comings and goings but from the indifference I'd encountered at the front gate, it was unlikely that they'd glean much.

I had questions of my own, particularly about White's mysterious backer. I did a quick search of the room and his belongings, poking through the drawers in the dressers, checking the pockets of his two jackets and three pairs of pants in the wardrobe, looking under the bed and flicking through the books and magazines. All the search told me was that someone else had done the job before me. Several of the pocket linings were displaced the way they get when the pockets are gone through, and the socks and underwear had been disturbed. There were no personal papers— insurance documents, letters, bills, photographs— but he could have had another storage place for them. The clincher confirming the previous search was that there was no wallet, no address book, no credit cards, no money—none of the things a person needs to get through the day.

There was a pay phone in the hallway near the kitchen, perhaps the phone White had used to call me. I dialled the emergency number, asked for the police and told my tale. I was instructed to stay where I was. There was no point in going anywhere. Frank Parker and Max Savage knew of my dealing with Barry White and would put two and two together when they heard of his death and they'd expect me to play it straight. I could expect some unpleasantness from the police but nothing I couldn't handle. They'd try to make me tell them what White and I were up to and I wouldn't. Our contract was locked in my safe and they'd need a pretty strong court order to get at it. They'd threaten me with obstruction and I'd tell them to see my lawyer, although I didn't actually have one. Perhaps I'd give them Wallace Cavendish's name.

The uniforms arrived first, then the detectives, then the forensic guys and lastly the body-movers. They took over the sitting room and I showed my

PEA licence and other ID to just about all of them it seemed, and told my story at least three times. They made me turn out my pockets and took the keys to my car for a look-see, but in general I was treated with more respect than usual—maybe because of the suit. The residents of the house were stirred up by the activity, some got agitated and there was a certain amount of anti-police aggression displayed. As my patience was stretched by the repetition, I began to enjoy that. Detective Sergeant Fowler eventually gave up a half-hearted effort at pressuring me and produced a pocket tape-recorder.

'How about you give me your statement, Mr Hardy? You seem to have the gift of the gab. I'll get it typed up and you can come in and sign it. Then we'll see what happens next.'

'Fair enough,' I said. I rattled off a strictly edited version of the events of the past few days while Fowler smoked, looked bored, and occasionally checked that the light on his recorder was still glowing. When I finished he hit the OFF button, butted his fifth or sixth cigarette and stood up.

'Right. Redfern station, let's say, three o'clock this afternoon, if that's convenient.'

'Sure. No complaint, but your attitude strikes me as a bit casual, Detective Sergeant.'

Fowler shrugged. 'Barry White was a fucking dog,' he said.

This development left me with what would have been an ethical dilemma if there were any hard and fast ethical rules in the PEA business. There aren't, not really. Of course you're supposed to have a client and a contract but no-one would blame me for pursuing the matter Barry White had brought to my attention and, if I ran into any sticklers for the letter of the law, I could always round up Leo Grogan as a stand-in. Of course, I was assuming that if White's death was connected with the Beckett inquiry, there was a certain amount of danger involved. There was the prospect now of a bigger cut of the reward to be considered. All in all, going on seemed worth the risk.

Sudden death can have curious and unexpected effects. I'd felt almost nothing on finding White, while searching his sad room and dealing with the police. But as I drove away I experienced something like a sense of loss, or a feeling about the transitoriness and futility of everything. A dark mood settled on me and, instead of heading back to the office and picking up the threads of the inquiry or getting in touch with Max Savage, I found myself driving down Glebe Point Road, heading for home. I had no idea of what I'd do there beyond have a few drinks and a walk in the park. I knew I wanted to get out of the suit.

I parked outside my house, edging in between my neighbour's Kombi van and a green Laser I hadn't seen in the street before. I got out and noticed a woman standing on the other side of the street looking intently at my house. She was tall and full-bodied in a stylishly cut charcoal grey suit. She wore a white blouse and her hair, almost the same colour, hung to her shoulders. She saw me looking at her and did a kind of double-take.

'Something wrong?' I said.

She crossed the street slowly and her leather shoulder bag swung slightly as she moved. 'I'm sorry,' she said, pointing at my shabby terrace. 'Is that your house?'

'Yes, it is.'

'I don't suppose you'd be interested in selling it?'

Every week I get circulars from real estate agents telling me how many buyers they've got for properties just like mine in the area, what prices they've fetched at auction for just such places, and how they'd be happy to help me sell. Some are cheap productions with blurred print, others have nice borders and clear, artistic photographs. Whatever, I put them all in the recycling bin. This was the first direct, human approach in that vein and it made a difference. The house looked bleak and neglected, the way I felt, but something about this woman—the animation in her face, the big, dark eyes and sculptured features—lightened my mood.

'I don't know,' I said. 'Could be. What agency are you from?'

She smiled. Great teeth. 'Oh, I'm not a real estate agent. It's just that I'm looking for a house in this part of Glebe. There's one on the other side a bit further down but I don't like it much, so I came up here just to scout about.'

We were standing quite close together now and I liked the sensation. Her perfume was pleasant and she had an easy grace that made me feel relaxed. 'I see,' I said. 'Well, houses come up from time to time. My name's Hardy, by the way, Cliff Hardy.'

Her hand came up naturally and we shook. 'Hi, I'm Claudia Vardon.'

Her accent was something like Greg Norman's Australian overlaid with American. Her hand was very dry, strong grip. No wedding ring. Her eyebrows were dark and her complexion was olive, making a startling contrast with the almost white hair. I guessed her age at about forty, but I'm a rotten judge of women's ages. I let go of her hand reluctantly.

'You say you just might be interested in selling, Mr Hardy?'

I shrugged. 'I think about it from time to time . . .' A car turned into the street and came around the bend too fast. We had to jump out of the way and we collided, hip to hip. I reached out to steady her and felt the firmness of her body.

'We don't get many hoons like that,' I said.

She wasn't rattled by the speedster, nor embarrassed by my touching her. Pleased, if anything. I was glad I was wearing my suit and had shaved carefully. 'How about the flight path?'

'Not too bad here. But we'll be getting a few planes soon. Would you like to have a look at the house? Chances are a plane'll go over and you can get the idea. Where do you live now, by the way?'

'In the city. Used to be Hunters Hill. The planes were terrible. Yes, all right, if it won't put you out.'

We went between my car and the Laser which

she nodded at. 'I cramped your parking space. Sorry.'

'That's OK.' I opened the gate and went ahead of her, pushing back some of the banksia that overhangs the path. The porch tiles have lifted where roots have got to them and there is a slight crack in the masonry from an old subsidence. If she noticed, she didn't comment. The house is cleaned twice a month by George and Shirley, a pair of local characters who do a good job, so that it smells OK but a bit musty from under-use. Claudia Vardon walked in confidently, peeked into the room off the hallway and gazed up the stairs. As luck would have it, sunlight streamed in through the skylight I put in a few years back and gave the upstairs a promising glow.

'Very nice,' she said. 'You haven't mucked it all up.'

'Far from it. It's pretty original. Two out of three fireplaces intact. No aluminium windows.'

She laughed. 'I hate those things.'

'Me, too. Look, put your bag down and have a good snoop through. I've had a tough morning and I'm going to make a sandwich and have a glass of wine. Would you like something?'

She slung her bag at a chair and it landed neatly. 'I've had lunch, thanks. Some wine would be great.'

I took off my jacket and headed for the kitchen. I heard her going up the stairs and grinned as she hit the step that squeaks like a mouse. I made a cheese and tomato sandwich, finished off the remainder of a bottle of Long Flat

White in two swigs and opened another. I had a glass poured for her when she came through to the kitchen.

'It's a good house,' she said. 'You've been here a while?'

'Mm. Have a drink.'

She took a solid sip. 'I don't think you want to sell this place. You and it seem to go together. I think you'd be lost anyplace else.'

I heard the low rumbling from above. I pointed at the ceiling. 'Hang on. Listen.'

We stood close together, almost touching, listening to the plane overhead. When it passed she touched me on the shoulder. 'Not bad at all.'

'No, that's about it. Come and have a look at the back.'

We carried our glasses out into the courtyard that I bricked in a rough fashion when Cyn and I first moved in here a hundred years ago. Grass grows through the cracks and some of the bricks have broken but it doesn't look too bad. Shirley waters the plants and pulls up some of the weeds. A biggish mulberry tree gives some shade and stains a section of the bricks. The plastic outdoor furniture is white-spotted with bird shit.

'If you stand on the fence you can see Black-wattle Bay,' I said.

She lifted one elegant black shoe. 'Not in these heels. It's a great place for you. Very spare, very masculine. D'you mind if I ask what you do for a living?'

'I'm a private detective. You?'

'I *was* a solicitor and should've stayed with it. I'm recently divorced, hence the great house search. The Hunters Hill place is sold and I'll get half—should be enough to buy something around here. I *love* Glebe even though it's changed. I lived here when I was a student at Sydney.'

We both drank wine. We both smiled. 'Will you go back into practice?' I said.

'Hell, I don't know. Why?'

'I need a lawyer.'

Her head went back and she laughed. I wanted to kiss her smooth brown throat. 'Does that mean you've got lots of money or lots of problems?'

'Prospects of both.'

'That's interesting. I'm not sure what I'm doing. I'm very rusty on everything, but we could talk about it.'

'Good. What're you doing tonight?'

She finished her wine and looked down at the glass. 'Nothing. Waiting.'

'Have dinner with me in Glebe. Indian, Lebanese, Spanish, French, Italian, you name it.'

'Why not?' she said. 'Indian sounds good. D'you think I should wear a sari?'

'You could,' I said. 'You could.'

9

I was as excited as a kid. Amazing how quickly and thoroughly that feeling of attraction to a new person of the opposite sex, when it's possibly reciprocated, can change your perspective and priorities. Claudia Vardon would be back at my house at 7 p.m. and I'd be ready. Barry White, Peggy Hawkins and the others in the cast of characters associated with the Beckett case all took two places to the rear. I was about to launch into a house-tidying, a bed-changing and buying some supplies when I remembered the appointment at Redfern station. The last thing I needed was a copper arriving on the doorstep that evening to conduct me to the lockup. I carefully hung the suit on a hanger, smoothed out the tie, checked that I had a clean shirt and socks and went off to Redfern in my more usual uniform of drill trousers, open-neck shirt and battered linen jacket.

Detective Sergeant Jack Fowler had evidently done a bit of checking up on me and was puzzled by the results. I was a long-term PEA and a mate of a well-placed senior cop and yet had recently served a prison sentence and been de-licensed for a period. Will the real Cliff Hardy please stand up? He conducted me to a room which wasn't as rough as the ones where they put the frighteners on the junkies nor as pleasant as where they interview child-molesting clergymen.

'We'd like to know more about your association with White,' he said.

'Sorry. Professional matter. Confidential.'

'You can't run that line.'

'I'm doing it. Look, all I can say is that the matter relates to events a good many years ago. Before you left school, Detective Sergeant. I have no reason to think White's death is connected to what we were discussing.'

'Discussing?'

'That's as far as it got.'

'You say you'd arranged to meet him at the house.'

'That's right.'

'Some of the blokes there say you seemed agitated.'

I knew that was a lie. The men who saw me arrive didn't register anything. 'I'm a busy man.'

'There was hardly a scrap of paper in the joint. No wallet, no TAB tickets, fuck-all.'

I shrugged. 'Your blokes patted me down. I didn't take a thing. I'd say that points to Barry's past history catching up with him. Someone cleaned up everything. What kind of gun was used?'

He looked at me, trying to gauge my honesty, sincerity, duplicity, but I'd been at this game longer than him and he gave it up. He took five sheets of printout from a folder and pushed them across the table. 'Sign it and you can go. You don't seem too cut up about losing your client.'

I hadn't brought a pen. I borrowed his blue ballpoint with a chewed end, read through the statement and signed at the foot of each page near the crosses. 'In the private sector, you learn to live with these disappointments. I hope you find out who did it. Any leads?'

He took back the sheets. 'Piss off,' he said.

Back home the red light on the answering machine was blinking reproachfully. I ignored it and set about putting the house in better order. I ran the gutless vacuum cleaner over the carpets, cleaned the bathroom and toilet and put out some fresh towels. I changed the sheets on the bed and three of the four pillow slips. I emptied the waste-paper baskets and the kitchen tidy and sprayed air freshener around where the air didn't smell fresh.

I wiped down the sink and bench tops, thought about pinching some flowers from other people's front gardens and decided against it. I ran a squeegee over the kitchen lino and took a few swipes at the coffee pot with steel wool. I'd bought wine and Scotch, biscuits and cheese, coffee and milk on the way home. Also mineral water, soap and shampoo and a packet of Trojan lubricated condoms. Be prepared.

I showered, shampooed and shaved as closely as my old electric Philishave would let me. I looked at myself in the mirror—the lines around the eyes are there for all time and getting deeper; the cheeks have long, parallel grooves in them where the dimples used to be. The only thing you could call an improvement is in the teeth which have brightened up since I stopped smoking and look better since I had the old decayed fillings replaced by ceramic stuff. Expensive but necessary. *You fool*, I thought. *She'll probably make a rock-bottom offer on the house and head for home when you turn it down.*

At seven-fifteen Claudia Vardon, wearing a blue silk dress and a white jacket, arrived at my door. An hour later the jacket was on the back of a chair at the Flavour of India restaurant in Glebe Point Road and we were looking at the menu and drinking Wolf Blass chablis. Two hours after that she took off the blue dress and her black underwear and lay down on my bed. Half an hour after that, give or take a few minutes, we were lying under the covers with sweat drying on us and our bodies still locked together and our hands still wandering.

'Jesus,' she said. 'I can still feel you in there.'

I pressed close to her and felt her muscles grip and hold me. 'I'm staying, too.'

'Can you come again?'

'I think so.'

'Go on, then, Cliff. Please go on. It's lovely.'

We did it again, less athletically but with more skill. I came in a long, almost painful shudder and didn't mind a bit when her fingernails sank into my shoulders.

'You didn't,' I said when I'd recovered.

'No. Catch you next time. Lovely, though. Lovely.'

I eased myself out of her and she put her hand down as I did, controlling the withdrawal. 'Easy, boy,' she said. 'Don't want any leaking. Let me do it.'

She rolled the condom off, reached for a couple of tissues, wrapped it up and dropped it on the floor. She brushed her hands together.

'That's it for *those* little Cliffords. *Are* there any little Cliffords or Cliffordettes by the way?'

'No,' I said. 'What about you?'

'Uh uh, left it till late in the piece and then I met Mr Wrong.'

'What would you like to drink?'

She moved away and slid out of the bed. 'A big glass of mineral water would be good, with lots of ice and just a little bit of wine. After I have a piss.'

I watched her as she headed for the bathroom. In the half-light her body looked dark and strong. Her waist was a bit thicker and her buttocks and hips fuller than current fashion dictated, but that meant nothing to me. I remembered the weight of her full breasts in my hand and the slight swell of her belly and felt myself getting hard again. I jumped up, wrapped a length of trade cloth brought back from New Guinea many years ago around me and went down to get the drinks. Her recipe sounded pretty good to me and I filled two schooners, but I had a decent swig of the wine as well, just for luck.

'D'you like being a private detective?' she said when I got back into bed.

I drank deeply. Her hand moved under the covers on to my thigh. Instantly, I forgot what she'd said a mere second ago. 'What?'

She laughed and took her hand away. 'Can't talk and get erect at the same time.'

'Try it again.' Her hand returned and stroked up towards my groin. 'Mostly I like it,' I said. 'Not as much as that, though.'

'Concentrate. Compartmentalise. Do you make a lot of money?'

'That's easy. In a word, no.'

'That's smart. Keep your responses short and you'll do fine.'

'I could turn the tables.'

'Why don't you?'

Things went on from there very pleasurably. We drank our mineral water and eventually fell asleep. Normally, I sleep deeply for the first few hours, then I get restless and often wake up and read for a while, fending off worries about money or what I'm working on at the time or deeper questions. The reading does the job, and I can mostly get back into a light sleep for a few hours. This night, despite its unusual features, was no different. I found myself awake at about 4 a.m., lying on my side with Claudia's arm across my waist. I was cramped and uncomfortable with a slight case of what used to be called shagger's back. It had been a while since I'd exercised those particular muscles, and a long time since I'd exercised them so thoroughly. She muttered something that might have been gibberish or in one of the many foreign languages I don't understand as she rolled into a new position.

I didn't want to read or to get up to drink water or piss or do anything, I was happy just to lie there with the warmth of her next to me. The street light is almost immediately outside the house and it penetrated the rice-paper blinds to some extent. The room wasn't in total darkness and I was able to examine Claudia's hair, spread out on the pillow beside me. It was thick and lustrous and quite white. As far as I could tell, it was the same colour from the tips to the roots. Curious.

She muttered again. The sheet fell away and I lifted it back to cover her smooth, brown shoulder. The softness of her skin was a delight and I found myself wanting to stroke her all over. I made do with kissing the shoulder. Her presence soothed and comforted me and I slid back into sleep without a thought of poor, dead Barry White or Max Savage or any of the rest of it.

'You haven't made me an offer on the house,' I said as Claudia and I drank coffee and ate toast in the courtyard.

She shook her head and the white hair flew. She was wearing just her blue lace petticoat with the white silk jacket over it and I was having difficulty keeping my eyes away from her breasts and legs. 'Like I said, you'll never leave unless they decide to put a freeway, or a bridge approach through it.'

'I've thought about Bondi.'

'You're not the Eastern Suburbs type. Too rugged.'

'So what're you going to do, Claudia?'

She took a good bite of toast and chewed enthusiastically. 'Keep looking for a house. Keep thinking about going back to work. How come you haven't got a lawyer?'

I told her about Cy and what had happened and she made sympathetic noises. She hadn't heard about it although it had made a big splash in the papers because she'd been overseas for most of the year, recovering from the break-up with her husband.

'So is Vardon the maiden or married name?'

'Detecting, are we?'

'Shit, sorry, no. I just . . .'

'It's OK. I'm a bit defensive, that's all. Vardon's *his* name. I'm going back to my name as soon as the settlement's through.'

Which was a way of saying don't ask too many questions. Glen Withers had said I exhausted her with questions and that I'd found out too much about her too soon. Left nothing to be surprised about and that was part of the trouble. I didn't believe it, but here was a chance to play it another way. I got on with eating toast and drinking coffee and let the moment pass, although it was hard to do. I wanted to ask where she grew up, what her husband did, about the white hair . . . Maybe Glen had had a point.

She finished eating and carefully brushed the crumbs from her plate into a pile on top of where the bricks are built up around the grapefruit tree so the birds could get them. 'You've gone quiet,' she said.

'Just keeping myself from being nosy. I've got to work today. Is it too pushy to ask if I can see you again tonight? I really want to.'

She got up from the plastic chair and squatted down in front of me. Her breasts were loose and heavy under the petticoat and I put my hands down and held them. Her face came up and we kissed hard.

'I like you more than your house,' she said. 'But I'm glad I stopped to take a look at it. Of course I want to see you, but you have to understand that I'm coming off a bad time, a couple of bad times. I don't trust my judgment.'

'Claudia, I . . .'

'Ssh. Don't come over all masterful. Men have to learn to let things happen. Now, you stay here and finish your coffee. Thank for a terrific night. I'm going to have a shower and then I'll go. I'll take down your phone number and I'll ring you soon. OK.'

It wasn't, but what could I do. Protest? Sulk? Reluctantly, I took my hands from her breasts. 'OK,' I said.

10

Well, I certainly wasn't going to sit around waiting for her to call. No percentage in that. I was eager to get up and go on the Beckett case, to be doing something so that romantic involvement didn't soak up all my energy and attention. That had happened a few times in the past with disastrous results—I either burnt the whole thing out too quickly or got let down badly. Not this time. I left the dishes in the sink, the empty bottle on the bench, the glasses where they sat and I didn't make the bed. I rang the number Max Savage had given me.

'Max Savage's phone.' A pleasant, young female voice, a big improvement on the usual response to a police number. Suddenly, I didn't quite know what to do next.

'Ah, my name's Hardy, Cliff Hardy. Can I . . . ah, leave a message for Mr Savage?'

'Max is here, Mr Hardy. I'm Constable Draper. I can act as relay between you if you wish.'

'Well, how does that work?'

I could hear a short, barking laugh on the line. Savage, for sure.

'You tell me what you want to say to Max and I'll tell him what you said. Then he speaks to you and you respond. It's very simple really. Just collect your thoughts.'

'Not very secure.'

'Don't be insulting. Do you want to talk to Max or not?'

'I'm sorry, Constable. Yes, please tell him I'd like to speed things up. I'd like a meeting today to work on the material we discussed yesterday.'

A pause, then Savage came on the line. 'Don't worry about Penny, Cliff, she's a heroine. I think we should get together today. Will Barry White's murder be on the agenda?'

'For sure, Max. I'm sorry if I offended her. Can you bring the notebooks?'

A pause, and I could hear Constable Penny Draper talking fast, verbatim as far as I could determine.

'Yeah,' Savage said, 'leastwise, photocopies of the interesting bits. What about your office in an hour and a half?'

'Will you be bringing Penny?'

I heard a peal of female laughter before she relayed what I'd said to Max.

Savage came back on the line and his voice was softer, without the cop edge. 'Penny's a paraplegic, Cliff. She got shot in the spine by some redneck dickhead who was beating the shit out of his girlfriend. She does the work of three people around her now. See, us handicapped aren't being tucked away in corners any more. No need to say anything. Your office, ninety minutes, OK?'

'OK,' I said. 'Thanks, Penny.'

'Have a good meeting.'

All of which left me feeling grateful that all my bits and pieces still worked despite the efforts a few people had made over the years to change that. I fetched the paper in from the front step and flicked through it. Barry White had made page three. A brief article, very light on for facts about his death, reviewed his inglorious career and implied that something from his past had surfaced and dragged him down. For all I knew, that could've been true.

Max Savage dumped a thick wad of photocopy paper on my desk and took the top off one of the two takeaway coffees I'd bought. 'That's for you,' he said. 'Any sugar?'

I reached into the bottom drawer, produced three packets and a wooden stirrer and passed them over. I rifled through the paper. 'Give me the gist.'

'Lazy bugger.' Max stirred briskly, sipped and sighed appreciatively. 'Ah, that's good. You must've had a big night?'

I was feeling a bit weary and hoped the long black I had would revive me. 'Why d'you say that?'

'Your face muscles are tired. You're not moving your mouth as much as usual when you talk. Makes it harder to read you.'

'Sorry,' I said, grimacing. 'That better?'

'Don't get shirty. Do you want to talk about this first, or about Barry White?'

It suddenly occurred to me that I'd lied comprehensively to one police officer and now was on the point of telling the truth to a man who was something like a cop himself. Max saw my hesitation and pointed his stirrer at me like a pistol.

'Let me guess, you didn't tell all to the Redfern Ds. And you're wondering where my priorities lie.'

I drank half of the very hot coffee in a gulp, hoping that it would give me a hit. 'Right.'

'It's an open case on my books. That's all I care about. Any perjury or misrepresentation by you doesn't interest me. How else could you operate? It's understood.'

Unbidden, an image of Claudia Vardon came into my head. She was getting back into bed after going to the toilet. Her whole body was silver-coloured in the dim light, like her hair. I'd forgotten that I'd seen this and I smiled. I felt better, despite a scalded tongue. 'Sorry, Max. I'm stumbling around a bit this morning. Right. I lied to Fowler. I said it was a prearranged meeting with Barry. It wasn't. He rang me in a panic. He needed help. No details. I was about half an hour too late. The other thing is, someone had been through his stuff before me and taken everything personal.'

Max nodded and finished his coffee. 'Ringing you suggests it was all to do with the Beckett case, but not necessarily.'

'The Beckett case could all be bullshit. Grogan's a drunk. He could be making it up. Maybe

Barry was just looking to hire some protection and it didn't quite work out.'

'Finish your coffee. It's doing you good. Nice try at devil's advocate, Cliff, but it won't wash. There's stuff in Hawkins' notebooks and the other reports on the file that back up what Grogan says.'

'Like?'

Max had changed his suit, shirt, tie and shoes from what he'd been wearing the day before. Only the briefcase was the same, and the keenness. 'How many police notebooks and internal memos have you seen?'

I grinned. 'I can think of a few I'd *like* to have seen, but I haven't actually seen any. None.'

'I've seen bloody thousands, a lot of 'em mine. I can read between the lines. Hawkins interviewed everybody—the father, the stepmother, the half-sister, the half-brother, the servants. He talked to everyone who sighted her in the last couple of days. But he didn't push anything. You can tell from the notes. He went through the motions, quite skilfully really, but it's there to see if you can read it. He was playing a dead bat.'

I thought about this. 'You said everybody— what about friends?'

'Ah, you've put your finger on something there. Not a single friend or acquaintance was talked to. Hawkins says that she didn't have any. That seems to me unlikely. He could be covering something up here.'

It sounded possible. Everyone has friends, don't they? Then an image of Ramona Beckett came to me: she was reaching out to tap ash off her cigarette. Her dress stretched tight over her hard, small breasts and the look on her face was predatory. Her style was to use people rather than befriend them. It was sad, but I could believe that she had no friends. 'What about a doctor?'

Max put the top back on his coffee cup and balanced the stirrer on top of it. 'Hawkins talked to the family GP. He hadn't seen her for years. Same with the dentist. As far as anyone knew she was in terrific health.'

'Yeah, that's right. Are you sure Hawkins didn't just get discouraged by running into all these negatives?'

'I'm sure.'

'Well, the next question is, on the basis of his investigation such as it was, can you make a guess at who might have nobbled Johnno?'

'No. Not really. He goes easy on them all. You'd expect that he'd be careful about that, wouldn't you?'

'This is not very helpful, Max.'

'Oh, I've been giving you the bad news. Get out your notebook. I've got a couple of names.'

I did as he said and stagily poised a pen over the page. 'Shoot!'

Max looked at me strangely. 'There's something different about you today. Are you given to big mood swings, hmm?'

'It's the thought that you're about to steer me towards that reward.'

'All right. Keep bullshitting. Now, you remember I was to look for anyone who might have

been in it with Hawkins? Well, there's two can-
didates. Colin Sligo and . . .'

'Sligo! Shit, I remember him. He was a hard
bastard. What happened to him?'

'He was a super at the time we're interested
in. He's a deputy commissioner of police in
Queensland these days. Due for retirement any
day.'

I wrote the name down. 'That's interesting.
And tricky.'

'All of that. The other starter is one Andrea
Neville.'

I wrote this in block capitals as well and
looked at the words. 'Doesn't ring a bell.'

'She was the policewoman who went with
Hawkins on his first visit to the Beckett house in
Wollstonecraft. It isn't clear from Hawkins' notes
who they saw first, but if it was the person with
an interest in suppressing the ransom note, they
were in the box seat to help out.'

'Come on, Max. That's stretching it.'

'I'm reliably informed that Neville was
Hawkins' girlfriend. About six months after the
Beckett case went quiet she resigned from the
force. I've asked around about her—the word at
the time was that she'd inherited a lot of money.'

'I see. Where is she now?'

Max shrugged. 'I'm working on it. Ex-coppers
can be tricky to find.'

'Right. Sorry for the scepticism, Max. This is
solid stuff. You must have been a hell of a good
detective.'

Max tapped his nose. 'I had a sort of an

instinct. I could smell things almost. Lucky that, because it's still there and it's helped me to cope with the hearing loss. Like, for instance, this new manner of yours . . .'

I laughed. 'OK, OK, you're right. I've met a woman and I'm keen on her, very keen. I'm hoping that something comes of it.'

Max smiled. 'Do you know, I'd have guessed it was something of the sort. Good luck to you. Now, about this matter on hand. I'd say your priority is locating Neville—that's worth a day or two. Failing that, or maybe leading on from that, we should talk to Peggy Hawkins a.s.a.p. . . . What's wrong?'

I shook my head. 'I'm used to working on my own. I'm *not* used to having a schedule laid out for me by someone else. Back off a bit, Max.'

He bit his lip and stared out of the window. He was a proud and stubborn man, struggling to overcome a disability, and backing down wouldn't be easy for him. But I meant what I said. My methods might be rough, even chaotic, but they've worked for me and I wasn't going to throw them overboard to suit Max Savage. Eventually he turned his head to look at me. 'Sorry. Still behaving like the boss. Consider me backed off. How d'you see things?'

'Supposing Barry White's death is connected to the Beckett case, I'm asking how do the lines of connection run?'

I was doing one of my diagrams as I spoke, writing names, circling and putting blocks around them and drawing arrows and dotted lines. Max half-rose from his chair to look at what I was doing. 'I see. Well, there's a few possibilities. Leo Grogan for one, though not very likely.'

'I've got him at the end of a broken line. I agree.'

'A leak at my end. Through Frank Parker or someone twigging to what I was doing with the files.'

I hadn't even entered Frank's name. 'Forget Frank. What about the other?'

Max shook his head. 'Not likely, but possible. The other connection is Barry White's backer. Let's say White reported back to him and the backer decided he'd roped you in and that was all he needed. That made White expendable. Against that, how would the backer get in for his cut without White?'

'Deal directly with me?'

'He'd have to convince you he hadn't offed Barry, wouldn't he? Mind you, that sort of money is pretty convincing.'

I looked at Max and he looked at me. 'I've had enough trouble lately without becoming an accessory to murder,' I said.

11

We agreed on an agenda. I would try to find out
who White had visited at the Connaught and get
on to Cavendish about seeing the members of the
Beckett family. I scrabbled among Harry Tickener's faxes for a newspaper article he'd thrown in
that contained a picture of Barry White. He was
slimmer then, but the grainy reproduction wasn't
flattering, and yesterday's Barry didn't look so
very different. It would do as a way of prompting
people. Max would check on the whereabouts of
Andrea Neville and find out all he could about the
present dispositions of Deputy Commissioner
Colin Sligo. As Max was leaving the phone rang
and I told him to stop, forgetting that with his
back turned he couldn't hear me. Of course, he
hadn't heard the phone ring. Simultaneously with
picking up the phone I tossed my styrofoam cup
in Max's direction. It hit him on the back of the
neck and he spun around.

'Hardy speaking.' I made a 'hang on' gesture
to Max who nodded, picked up the cup and
dropped it into the waste-paper bin.

'This is Wallace Cavendish, Mr Hardy. I've

spoken to Mrs Beckett and she has agreed to see you. Would six-thirty today be acceptable?'

I hesitated for a fraction of a second. It had the sound of a time when Claudia might ring, but there was no way to know and I'd resolved not to let anything about her faze me. 'Certainly, Mr Cavendish. Thank you for your cooperation. I take it you'll be there?'

'Most definitely. Let me give you the address.'

He rattled off an address in Wollstonecraft, not a part of Sydney where I spend much time. A *Gregory's* job. I scribbled it down. 'Thanks. At six-thirty then.'

'Please be prompt. Mrs Beckett doesn't like to be kept waiting.'

'I'm the same,' I said. 'I'll be there.' I rang off and looked at Max, who was shifting his weight from side to side impatiently.

'Cavendish,' I said. 'I'm seeing the old girl this evening. Sorry about chucking that at you. I just didn't know how else to get your attention and I thought it might be important.'

'That's OK,' Max said. 'The whole bloody deafness thing just pisses me off sometimes. What're you going to say to her?'

I shrugged and took a chance. 'I'll play it by ear.'

Max threw back his head and roared. 'Good one, Cliff. Good one. I'll be in touch.'

The day was clear and bright with a bit of autumn in the breeze. It can be the best time of the year in Sydney, when warm days give way to cool nights. In the past people could sunbake, if they could get out of the wind, until May. Now they don't do that much and, anyway, the wind would blow their hats off as they were heading for the sheltered spots on the beach. I bought three pieces of fruit in a shop in William Street, averted my eyes from the pubs, and headed for the Connaught.

For some reason Whitlam Square, a five-ways, is one of the windiest places in the city. It was blowing hard and the dust was flying when I arrived and I had my head down and my eyes almost closed as I went up the ramp towards the entrance to the Connaught. I was aware of someone in front of me but I was floundering, blinking against the dust, when we collided.

'You bastard!'

I stumbled back and was three metres below her when I finally got my eyes open. Claudia Vardon stood there looking as if she'd shoot me if she had a gun. She was wearing a white dress that emphasised the smooth brown of her skin. Her hair was blowing wildly in the wind and her right fist was clenched.

'You followed me here! You goddamn snoop!'

'Claudia, no, I swear I didn't. This is a coincidence. I'm here tracking someone. A man. Jesus . . .'

'Coincidence, come on.'

People were looking at us as we stood, three steps apart, voices raised, arguing. I went up the steps and tried to take her arm. 'Let's get away from here so we can talk. I can prove to you that

I didn't follow you. I wouldn't. I respect your privacy.'

She shied away from my touch but she let out a deep breath and seemed to soften a little. 'You're right. We can't talk here.'

'Is there a coffee shop or something?'

She nodded and led the way down to a coffee shop cum deli on what was called the Connaught Concourse. When we were seated I reached into my pocket for the photo of White. 'This guy hired me a couple of days ago.'

She barely glanced at the photo. 'To do what?'

'To investigate something.'

'Of course. And . . .'

'I didn't quite trust him, or rather I wanted to know more about him, so I followed him after another meeting and he came in here. I was going to show this picture around and ask if anyone had seen him.'

'He lives here?'

'No, no. He's got some kind of benefactor who might live here. I want to find out who that is.'

The waitress came over and we ordered coffee.

'Why can't you ask him who this benefactor is?'

'He wouldn't tell me. Anyway, he's dead now.'

Her huge, dark eyes opened wide and I could feel the anger going out of her as a more important matter was on the table. 'But you said yesterday . . .'

'He was killed yesterday, just a few hours before I met you.'

The coffee came and I found myself telling her almost everything about the case, leaving out most of the names. I wasn't trying to impress her, more trying to convince her that I hadn't snooped. She listened and asked the odd question and I was aware again of how sharp her mind was and I could sense that there was a lawyer in her, just below the surface. She stopped the flow by putting her hand on my arm.

'It's OK, Cliff. I believe you.'

'Good. Thank you. This is all a bit weird, Claudia. I've been thinking about you non-stop. The bloke I'm working with, this Max I mentioned, says I'm a different man today.'

She spooned up froth from her cup. 'Oh, yeah. And just what have you been thinking about me?'

I covered her hand with mine and then I interlaced our fingers. She didn't object. 'I respect your . . .'

'Right to privacy. You said that. Anyway, it's blown. I live here, temporarily.'

'I was going to say your caution.'

She laughed. 'Do you call last night cautious.'

'No, I call it bloody wonderful.'

'So do I. Come up to my place.'

Her apartment was on the eighth floor with a great view across the park towards the water. I didn't get much more than a glimpse of it over her shoulder because we were clawing at each other within seconds of getting inside. She had white, lacy things under the white dress and some of them stayed on as we thrashed around on her bed. We kissed so hard it was like two boxers locking heads, and her tongue in my mouth and her hands down below quickly had me up and ready to go. She knelt on the tight pink satin sheet and shoved me onto my back. She hovered over me like a great white-crested, brown-plumaged bird. Then she swooped down and took me in her mouth.

I fought for control as I ran my hands over her firm body, kneading the flesh of her buttocks and breasts and thrusting my fingers into her. I was close to exploding when she left off and, still gripping me with one hand, fumbled in a drawer. She rolled the condom on and mounted me in what seemed like one smooth motion. She guided my hand around behind her and put my finger up into her anus as she bore down on me.

'Now you hold on,' she said. 'For as long as you can.'

She rode me, knocking the breath from me with her weight. I reared up and it felt as if I'd never been so deeply inside a woman before. She was moaning and twisting on top of me and it was painful and blissful at the same time. She increased the tempo, found the rhythm she wanted and went on and on until she came in a long, heaving rush that brought me helplessly to my climax and had me shouting something up into her dark, beautiful face. She collapsed, slipped sideways and I slid out of her but grabbed her with both hands and pulled her close, wanting to feel the whole length of her against me.

'Jesus,' she said. 'Oh, Jesus.'

I said nothing, just clung to her and struggled against a mad impulse to weep and laugh at the same time. I could feel myself shaking and she pushed back against me.

'Cliff, what's wrong? Are you having some kind of fit?'

'No, no. It was just so good. So good.'

She rolled away; the condom had come free and semen or lubricant or both was on her thigh. She stood beside the bed smiling down at me. She had pulled the cover off and the top sheet down before we started, now she lifted the sheet up over me and shoved a pillow under my head. She unhooked her bra. Her large brown nipples were erect and I reached out to touch the nearest one.

She slapped my hand away. 'Enough. Have a little sleep, why don't you. I'm taking a shower.'

My body was hot and the pillow and sheets were cool. I was weightless, floating, and I was asleep before she got her stockings off.

When I woke up she was sitting at the end of the bed looking at me. She was wearing a floor-length white satin robe, modestly closed across her chest. It's an odd feeling to wake up with someone watching you. Did you dribble or say something you shouldn't have? I must have looked troubled.

'Why are you looking like that?' she said.

'Like what?'

'There was a sort of angry look on your face.'

'I dunno. I sort of thought how vulnerable a sleeping person is to one who's awake.'

She laughed. 'Jesus, that's paranoia if ever I heard it. I suppose it goes with the job. Makes it a bit hard on your women, though.'

'You're right there. I'm not good at hanging on to women, or they're not good at hanging on to me. I suppose trust has something to do with it.'

'We'll see. Where d'you want to go from here, Cliff?'

'On,' I said.

'Me, too.' She crawled along the bed to me and I reached for her and we lay with our arms around each other. She smelled of shampoo and I stroked the fine, strong white hair.

'Wondering about that?' she said.

'A bit, but I like it. It's beautiful hair.'

'It's one of those things you read about but it actually happened to me. I had red hair, well, dark red. I was in a car crash once. Not too serious, cuts and bruises and concussion, but I saw what was going to happen before it did and got the fright of my life. My hair turned white while I was in the hospital. Not overnight, but over a couple of weeks. I dyed it for years but now I like it this way. You don't think it makes me look old?'

'Couldn't.'

'Thank you. Well, we've made some progress. We're great in bed, and we both like curry. I wonder what else we might be able to do together?'

'Travel, maybe?'

'That's a thought. Where?'

'Paris?'

'Jesus, this is speeding up. What . . .?'

I'd looked at my watch on the bedside table. It was after five. It felt as if I'd had ten minutes sleep and it was more like a couple of hours. I moved in the bed and she detached herself.

'I'm sorry,' I said. 'I have to see someone pretty soon.'

She patted my shoulder. 'That's OK. Who?'

'Ramona Beckett's mother.'

'Well, that'll be interesting for you. What . . . never mind.'

'Go on.'

'I was going to ask you what line you'd take with her, but it's none of my business. I just wish I had something as interesting as that to do myself, instead of just waiting for this bloody settlement to come through.' She jackknifed off the bed like a gymnast. 'You'd better have a shower. Can't go calling on an elderly lady smelling like that.'

I showered and dressed. She had a bottle of white wine open when I came out to the living room and she put a glass in front of me. 'Tell you what. Give me that picture you had and I'll ask around about him. I know how this place works.'

I was doubtful but I took out the photo. 'What will you say?'

'What would you have said?'

'It'd depend on who I was talking to.'

'Well, likewise. Anyway, the security in this place is so tight you'd get nowhere. Do you realise our keys only allow us to access our own floors and the roof? That's where the pool and spa and saunas are. And the gym. At least I can ask around in the lifts and the public spaces.'

I handed the photo to her. 'OK, thanks. That could be a big help, but you have to promise you won't follow it up if you get a bite.'

'No way. I'll just tell you next time we meet, which will be when?'

'Tomorrow.'

'Yes. Can I come to your office? You've invaded my inner sanctum, I wanna get a look at yours.'

We agreed to meet there at noon. I finished the drink. We stood up simultaneously and kissed.

'I would've called you, Cliff,' she said. 'Just about now.'

12

Wollstonecraft is not that far from Glebe as the shark swims, but it's a million miles away in atmosphere and economics. I got out of the car to walk about, kill a few minutes and take in the ambience. The first thing that struck me was the quiet. A few cars purred by but otherwise the only sounds were from birds in the trees and garden sprinkler systems. A telephone booth I passed held a full set of intact directories—White and Yellow Pages.

As I negotiated my way to the Beckett house I reflected that the middle classes have apparently held out here against change. Their big houses still sit on big blocks with high fences and hedges. No granny flats and subdivisions. Apartment buildings have gone up, particularly near the railway station, but they were all solid and gracious, like the houses—high-rent places, not likely to attract anyone who might let down the tone. The migrant influx must have had an affect on the commercial life of the suburb, but my guess was that it hadn't changed the domestic patterns. The word Waterloo was sculptured into a hedge. *That'd be right*, I thought, *Anglophiles'd be thick on the ground around here*. I wondered how Gabriella Vargas had fitted in. She must've liked it, hadn't moved.

The house was probably the best one in the best street, a cul-de-sac with bushy parkland along one side and at the bottom. It looked out across a stretch of reserve towards Balls Head Bay. Behind the three-metre hedge I could see the top levels of the elegant sandstone mansion and the word villa came to mind. On a good day you'd have a great view of the yachts on the water from up there and be breathing air that would have less lead, carbon monoxide and other poisons in it than that inhaled by most Sydney residents. There were only two cars in the street, visitors, obviously. Here, you drove through your gates and tucked your Merc up snugly for the night in your garage or car port. I checked my watch. Six-twenty. She didn't like people being late. I wondered how she felt about early.

I pressed a button on the gatepost, announced myself and pushed the gate open after the click. The front garden was a nice blend of paving stones, grass, shrubs and flower beds. There were a couple of benches situated where shade would fall at the right times of day. I went up three sandstone steps to the wide front porch and pressed another button, plenty of index-finger exercise in this neck of the woods. The door was opened by a small woman in a dark dress with a white collar. In the old days she'd have been able to take my hat, cane and gloves, now she just had to show me to the room where Cavendish and Mrs Beckett were waiting. I was still six minutes early.

Drapes were drawn against the still strong outside light and the room was gloomy. An eye injury I suffered a few years back has slowed down my ability to adapt from light to dark. I'd have to be careful not to bump into the furniture. Cavendish stood beside a chair in which Gabriella Beckett sat. It was hard to see her clearly in the poor light. Perhaps that was the idea, but I got an impression of great beauty and great sadness. As I got closer I could see that her skin was dark and drawn tight over high cheekbones. Her nose was slightly hooked and her eyes were deeply sunk or maybe only seemed that way because of the nose. Her hair was white with a creamy tinge. She wore a black lace dress with long sleeves; she looked to be tallish, but if she weighed fifty kilos that'd be all.

'Good evening, Mr Hardy,' she said. Her voice was slightly accented, hitting the middle syllables.

'Mrs Beckett. Good of you to see me.' I nodded at Cavendish.

'Let's make this brief, Hardy. Mrs Beckett isn't well.'

'I'm sorry to hear that.' Apart from being too thin she looked fine to me. I struggled to see a resemblance to Ramona but it was too long ago for me to have a clear picture.

'Please sit down, Mr Hardy. I understand you have certain information about the circumstances surrounding my daughter's disappearance.'

I sat in one of the rather severe chairs arranged around a low table in the middle of the room. I was only two metres away from her now and fancied I could see what old Josh had gone for. Almost old, she was striking, when young she must have been stunning.

'That's right. And certain questions.' I wanted to cut Cavendish out of the exchange as much as possible and the easiest way to do it was to refer to him as if he wasn't there. It sometimes works. 'Has Mr Cavendish briefed you?'

'Partly. I'm hoping you can be more frank with me than you were with him.'

Cavendish moved away from her chair and sat across from us where he could observe her perfect profile and my battered one. I couldn't see any reason not to tell her what I was about and I did. Having told it all to Claudia just recently, I could lay it out succinctly. I didn't mention Barry White's murder though.

'It's possible,' she said.

Cavendish leaned forward. 'Gabriella . . .'

She fended him off with an imperiously raised forefinger. 'Sean and Estelle both hated Ramona. She gave them reason. She was far more attractive and much more intelligent than they. Her father adored her, of course. She was a difficult child and, I have been led to believe, a dangerous woman. But she was interesting, unlike the other two.'

It all sounded a bit clinical to be coming from a grieving mother, but then, it was a long time ago. 'Are you saying it's possible one or both of them could have worked with the investigating officer to repress a ransom note and so cause Ramona's death?'

She shook her head slightly, not enough to disarrange the creamy white hair. 'No. They certainly wouldn't have acted together. They dislike each other almost as much as they hated Ramona. Wallace mentioned your question about the police and it set me thinking. Sean and Sergeant Hawkins were similar types—beer and horses men. Sean lacked courage but the policeman may have supported him.'

'Estelle?'

The corners of her mouth turned down. 'Far too stupid to do anything beyond check a hem length and advise on a flounce. I have to say that her success in the fashion business just proves what mindless nonsense it all is.'

'What does Sean do now?'

'He's on the board of four of his father's companies and owns stock in them and others. He draws massive fees and dividends and does nothing to earn them.'

Cavendish was shaking his head but she ignored him as I had hoped she would. I said, 'But you don't know anything that points directly to Sean being involved?'

For the first time she began to look tired and I was able to believe that perhaps her health wasn't good. She clasped and unclasped her long fingers and worked at the thin wedding ring. 'No, nothing,' she said. 'But Sean bitterly opposed the announcement of a reward. He even argued with his father about it, something he almost never did. Of course, Joshua won. He always won. Always.'

There were things to explore here, but Cavendish had had all he could take of being cut out. He stood and towered over us both. 'I think that's enough, Hardy. You've covered the ground you said you wanted to explore. Enough.'

'Wallace tells me that you are a capable man, Mr Hardy. With a reputation for violence and honesty. That's an unusual combination. Ramona combined unusual elements in her character, too. Perhaps you are the person to unravel the mystery.'

The sadness was stronger in her now than the beauty and I got up slowly, more in response to that than to Cavendish's bluster. She held out her hand and I took it. It was cold and I could feel the bones in her fingers. 'Learn all you can, Mr Hardy. I still want to know what happened to my child.'

Cavendish escorted me to the door and came through it with me. He waved the servant off and stayed beside me on the longish walk to the front door, which he opened with an easy familiarity.

'Looks like I'd better have a word or two with Sean,' I said. 'I don't suppose you'd facilitate that as well?'

Cavendish shook his head. 'I think you should drop it altogether.'

'Why's that?'

'For Gabriella's sake.'

'I think she wants me to pursue it.'

'You're trading on an old woman's vulnerability.'

I wanted to hit him. The words had tripped off his tongue so easily. I couldn't have come up with such a glib phrase, but I felt sure that it described precisely what *he* was doing. 'She's not so old,' I said. 'And I don't think she's all that vulnerable.'

'You don't know her,' he said. His body language tried to ease me through the open door but I resisted.

'That's the funny thing,' I said. 'I almost feel as if I do.'

'What do you mean?'

'I don't know.'

'Look, Hardy. You may have given her something to latch onto for a while. But it's a fantasm and you know it. If you would agree to let all this fade away quietly I could be of some help to you. Not to put too fine a point upon it, I could perhaps put some remunerative work your way.'

I looked at him. He was overdressed for the day and sweating slightly, but not only because of the suit. His hair stuck to his skull, his face was redder than it had been, and he looked agitated. I took two quick steps away and left him in exactly that state, feeling that the interview had really been quite productive. I took a quick look back at the house before I opened the front gate. Cavendish still stood in the open doorway and he was talking into a mobile phone.

I drove down the cul-de-sac, intending to make a

turn and come back. I was committed to this before I noticed the two cars that had cruised up behind me, forming a solid block across the road. They were four-wheel drives with bullbars, the right vehicles for the job and they jammed me against the gutter at the bottom of the street. Two men got out of the blue Land Cruiser and a third from the red Pajero with silver mudflaps. They weren't there to discuss insurance or bring me to Jesus. The guy from the Pajero carried an aluminium baseball bat and the others just had their chests and shoulders and that looked like enough. I reached under the seat as I got out and grabbed the length of lead pipe I'd acquired when the tribunal that had returned my PEA licence added the proviso that I was not to carry a firearm. I'd wound red insulating tape around the pipe to give it a grip and a serious look, but right then I'd have preferred my Smith & Wesson .38.

They knew their business. One of them circled around to cut off a dash into the park and the others pressed forward, herding me towards the edge of the reserve where the trees cast deep shadows. If I retreated. I stood my ground for a second or two and then moved up to the nearest of the 4WDs, using it to protect my back.

'Won't help you, Hardy,' the bat man said. He was medium-sized, compact, a dangerous middleweight.

I glanced up the street. No help from that direction. The trees in the gardens of the big houses blocked any view of this spot.

I swung the pipe. 'I can put a dint in that toy

of yours though, and in your fucking skull if you get close enough.'

'Tough talk.'

'Let's try it.'

His jaws were moving rhythmically as he chewed gum. 'I don't think so.'

He raised the bat and I reacted, tightening my grip on the pipe, but it was only a feint. He flicked the bat from one hand to another. I knew enough about this sort of thing not to watch, to look for something else, but I was too slow. I was aware of a sweeping movement to my left, a throw. I tried to duck but something heavy and hard caught me above the left ear and I went down in a heap. I kept my grip on the pipe though and when a leg came into my field of very blurred vision, I swung at it and felt a satisfying crunch.

'You cunt!'

A boot crashed into my elbow and the pipe was gone. The bat landed close to where the thrown object had and I felt sick in the head and stomach and legs. I could feel blood dripping down the side of my face.

'Easy,' a voice said.

I was face-down and going under and couldn't turn to look, but the kick to the ribs didn't seem to be in response to the command. Neither did the next kick on the other side or the next thump to the head. I had a sudden, irrational fear for my expensive dental work, but I needn't have worried. The next pain I felt was in my scalp. A hand was gripping my hair and lifting my head up. I smelt Juicy Fruit.

114

'A taste, Hardy. Just a taste. Give it up!'

I scarcely felt the next blow that blotted out all light and sound and feeling.

13

Sweat running into the corners of my eyes and stinging woke me up. I blinked and the stinging got worse, then receded. I was sitting in the passenger seat of my car outside my house. It was 8.33 on the car clock and dark. My head throbbed and I was soaked with sweat the way my diabetic mother sometimes got when she took too much insulin or didn't eat. I could remember her dress being wringing wet as we helped her out of a chair and my father took her into the bathroom. She smelt of gin or sherry or both and she'd murmur about how sorry she was. I was sorry myself, but I was sober. The sweating was a reaction to what I was pretty sure was concussion.

My throat felt as dry and rough as a sheet of bark and I wanted water badly enough to make me consider moving. I turned my head slightly and the pain shifted around a bit but didn't get worse. I put my hands on the dashboard and my ribs on both sides screamed but no bones grated. I became aware that the steering lock was on and that my car keys were in my lap. I moved my feet and felt something on the floor. Slowly I reached down for it and the keys fell. I picked them up and scrabbled for whatever it was I'd felt. My fingers touched the taped grip of the pipe and I lifted it. That was easy to do in the confined space because it had been bent into a rough circle. Nice touch.

Getting out of the car wasn't too hard. Standing up was harder but do-able. The first step felt like it does when you've been in bed for days with the flu—not quite real, the ground spongy underfoot. I pushed off from the car and let the door swing closed. The sound it made bounced around inside my skull like a stone in a hubcap. I rested at the gate for a bit, then used the low brick fence to grope my way up the path to the front door. *Drunk again*, anyone watching might have said, but that would have been very unfair. I couldn't remember the last time booze had made me feel this bad. I made it inside, turning on lights and shutting my eyes against them, and back to the kitchen where I drank three big glasses of water, one after another.

I could feel dried blood in my hair and on my neck and I went into the bathroom to inspect the damage. The face I saw in the mirror was pale except where blood had dried in a smear all down the left side. My left ear had felt odd the whole time and now I could see why. A gauze pad had been taped to it. I lifted the edges of the tape and tried to move the pad but it was glued on with blood which started to ooze out. Better left alone. I washed the blood from my face and used a soapy cloth to scrub it gently from my hair, being very gentle with the tender area above the ear. The effort made me dizzy and I sat down on the edge of the bath. I ran the water, stripped off my sweaty clothes and eased myself in. I had bruises up the ribs and a swelling on one elbow.

As the warm water soothed me I reflected on the experience. I've had a few bashings in my time but this was the strangest. What kind of a strongarm man says 'Easy' when he's hardly started and does running repairs after the damage? And drives you home? Considering the baseball bat and the blow I'd landed with the pipe, I'd clearly got off very lightly. The badly bruised ribs made getting out of the bath difficult. I resolved one thing—I was going to carry the .38 from now on. Fuck the tribunal.

After a bad night I creaked my way around to Ian Sangster's surgery and got him before he opened shop. Ian is an old friend and one of those doctors who smokes and drinks, eats old-fashioned Aussie tucker, stays up late and doesn't exercise. He's showing the wear and tear now, but his view is that anything is better than Alzheimer's and that his lifestyle is the sure preventative. When I arrived he was butting out probably his fifth cigarette and sipping his fourth cup of strong coffee.

'Jesus Christ,' he said. 'It's the St John's Ambulance practice dummy.'

'Hah, hah. Take a look at me will you, Ian? And tell me I'm going to live.'

He lit another cigarette. 'We're none of us

going to live, Cliff. I thought I'd taught you that. What happened?'

I shrugged and immediately wished I hadn't. Most things hurt. 'Baseball bat, boot, things like that.'

He smelt bad but his touch was soft and soothing. He helped me off with my shirt and from somewhere produced a spirit-soaked cloth and sponged away the dressing on the ear. 'That needs a stitch or two,' he said, 'but baseball bat and boot . . . I'd say he wasn't trying.'

'They, Ian, they!'

'Oh, of course. Six was it, seven?'

I winced as he swabbed the wound and started stitching. 'Three's usually enough. Was this time. I might have busted an ankle with a bit of lead pipe.'

'Hold still! Does doing that make you feel any better?'

'My oath it does.'

'They that live by the sword . . . That's a bad knock above the ear, but luckily you've got a skull like a rock. It should go into a museum. I'll see to it if you like.'

'Fuck you. I can see and hear all right. D'you reckon I had a concussion?'

He disposed of his surgical gear and picked up the cigarette. After a deep drag he examined my eyes. 'In your case, hard to tell. Your brain's banged against the cranial vault so often they might've fused. Mild, I'd say, at worst. Take a deep breath.'

I sucked in wind and gasped at the sudden

shaft of pain. 'Mmm, cracked probably,' he said. 'Be a good idea to bind them up since I don't suppose you're planning to spend the next week taking it easy?'

'I have to work for a living. I can't just send in Medicare forms and lie back perving on nurses.'

He ran about twenty metres of bandage around my trunk and taped it into place. 'There you go, Cliff. A few pain-killers which I'll prescribe and you're ready to commit more violence on your fellow citizens. Tell you one thing, though.'

'What's that?'

'You'll have a bit of trouble fucking in the missionary position.'

When I got home there was a message from Max Savage's offsider to ring a.s.a.p.

'Penny Draper.'

'Ms Draper, this is Cliff Hardy.'

'Oh, yes, Mr Hardy. I'll put Max on.'

'Cliff, Max. No point in all that polite stuff, I'd just have to give the phone to Penny. I've found Andrea Neville. I think we should go and have a chat with her.'

'This is Penny. Respond, please.'

'Yes. Where? When?'

'You're a natural, you've picked up the style real quick,' Max said. 'She's running an art gallery in Paddington, would you believe. Trumper Place, number six. Southern Cross Gallery. See you there in half an hour.'

I've lived in Sydney all my life and I'm still coming across places, quite close in to the city, that I've never been to. I climbed tentatively into the car, established that I'd be able to drive with a bit of discomfort, and consulted the *Gregory's*.

Trumper Place was tucked in between the flats of Edgecliff and the terraces of Paddington. Trumper Park was an eye-opener: the tiny oval was like something out of the last century with an immaculate white picket fence all around and grassy surrounds for the spreading of rugs and the eating of cucumber sandwiches. It didn't look as though it'd be hard to hit a six from the pitch in the centre but distances from the perimeter can be deceptive. One incongruous note was that the ground was set up for the playing of Australian football. Two or three joggers circled the oval. I felt as if I was looking simultaneously at the past, the present and the future.

There were two galleries, one a big, elaborate affair in a newish building and the one we were interested in, very much its poor cousin—a terrace house, painted in grey and white, but not recently. Automatically, I scouted around to see if there was a back entrance. There wasn't, all traffic went through the front. I stood outside and watched Max's taxi draw up.

'What happened?' Max said when he was still a couple of metres away.

I was sure he couldn't see the stitches in my ear and there were no other visible signs of the bashing. I stared at him. 'What d'you mean?'

'You've had an accident. You're holding

yourself stiffly, protecting ribs I'd say.' He got closer and saw the ear. 'That looks nasty.'

'I'll tell you all about it later. How do we play this? Have you got any kind of police authority?'

'You must be joking. No, we're both in pretty much the same boat. This place is run by Andrea Craig, née Neville, and Eve Crown. Lesbians by all accounts.'

I looked at the drooping bamboo plants in two big pots sitting on cracked concrete slabs in the front of the house. The two-storeyed terrace was narrow and built in the skimpy fashion that takes a lot of the charm away from the style— minimum wrought iron, plain paving, uncovered porch. 'Doesn't look too prosperous,' I said.

Max snorted. 'It's a front.'

'For what?'

Max wandered up the street towards the oval and I followed. 'That Penny's a remarkable young woman,' he said. 'She's been putting fizzgig stuff on a data base for a couple of years. You wouldn't believe what she's come up with.'

'The computer's putting me out of business, Max. I don't want to hear about its wondrous mysteries. Just fill me in on the fucking art gallery.'

'Right.' Max pulled out a notebook and began flipping over the pages. 'No significant exhibitions or sales in the last eight years. What does that suggest to you?'

'Lousy art, lousy promotion or cash flow from somewhere else.'

'Exactly. In this case, from what we can

gather, they peddle a high-class line of pornography. You can get your portrait painted in any style you like, wearing whatever clothes you like or none at all and keeping company with whoever you fancy likewise.'

'Sounds harmless enough.'

'I understand some of the portraits are real life studies and that some of the subjects clients choose are very young and some of the posing sessions are . . . realistic.'

'Oh, shit. Why hasn't anything been done about it?'

Max shrugged. 'No complaints laid, all very discreet. But I don't think we have to be too gentle with the ladies.' He took a newspaper clipping from his pocket and studied it. 'We're here to see an exhibition of the photography of Robyn McKenzie. I understand she's very good. Are you interested in photography?'

'No.'

'Neither am I.'

We went back to the terrace and Max pressed the buzzer. 'Is it ringing?' he asked.

I got closer to the door. 'No. Nothing.'

'Strange. Place's supposed to be open now.'

He gave the door a tentative push and it swung in. We walked immediately into a big airy space. The wall that usually forms the passage in a terrace had been taken out and the front room was open right back to the stairs. It was filled with light from the front and side windows; the board floor was polished and framed photographs hung

123

around the walls. Through the archway was a second room in the same condition. We walked through to a couple of small rooms at the back which were evidently offices. The photographs were black-and-white studies of buildings, none of them familiar to me.

Max stood at the foot of the stairs and raised his voice. 'Hello! Anybody about!'

I heard noises upstairs, feet shuffling, a nose being blown, a clink of glass and the snap of a cigarette lighter. A figure appeared on the upstairs landing where there wasn't much light. A plume of smoke drifted down to us.

'What the hell do you want?'

Max turned to me and I mouthed the words to him, adding 'A woman'.

'We want to see Andrea Craig,' Max said.

A harsh, cigarette-tortured laugh sounded and she came slowly down the stairs. She was tall and thin with long, thick hair sprinkled with grey. She wore a silk dressing gown only loosely fastened so that most of her breasts were showing. Her pale face was lined and haggard, her eyes red-rimmed from weeping.

'You and me both,' she said. 'She's gone. She's fucking left me.'

14

'We've been together for eight years. Then she gets one phone call and she's off. No explanation, nothing. She said she'd send for me but I know all about that. She must've been seeing someone else for ages and it finally all came good. Lying bitch.'

Eve Crown needed to talk and Max and I were as good as anyone else, maybe better than most. I told her I was a private detective and that Max was 'with the police'. A glint came into her eyes and she took us upstairs to the flat she and Andrea Craig had shared and she showed us the clothes and other items strewn around in a super-hasty packing. Some of the clothes were torn and a couple of pictures had the glass in them broken. One was a photograph of a blonde woman with a narrow face, small mouth and enormous eyes. Then we sat around a table in the kitchen that had been remodelled in the fifties and hadn't changed since—laminex and lino, cupboards with plastic ventilation insets.

'We fought a bit, but she's stronger than me

and she knows about those things. She was a policewoman once.'

Max was having a lot of trouble following what she said. She smoked continuously, lighting one from the butt of the last. She mumbled, dropped her head and the hair fell across her face when she looked up. She didn't need much prompting but it was up to me to keep her talking. She didn't even ask what our business was; she was setting an agenda of her own.

'I suppose you're onto us about the pictures and all that?' she said.

'Among other things,' I said. 'But we're mostly concerned to talk to her about something back in her police days.'

This time she butted the cigarette she was smoking and paused to wipe ash from the front of her dressing gown, modestly closed now, before lighting another one. 'You'll go looking for her?'

'Yes.'

'Good. I'll give you enough to put her in gaol.'

Max was looking pained at being shut out of the conversation, as well as impatient, and I said, 'Look, Miss Crown. Could you please tell us when this phone call came and exactly what she said and did.'

She flicked ash at the saucer serving as an ashtray and scored half a hit. Her fingernails were bitten down on her non-smoking hand. 'Last night, late,' she said. 'About eleven I suppose. She was in bed and I was doing the books for the quarter. I do all the work around here. I answered the phone. It was for Andrea and I switched it through. Then all hell broke loose.'

She dragged on the cigarette while she spoke and Max was stymied. Speaking clearly, I said, 'A male voice or female, local call or STD?'

'Shit, I don't know. Some of us dykes go in for deep voices, you know? Like the gays have that lilt? I couldn't say.'

'Accent?'

'I can't remember. It didn't register. I don't think I heard any beeps. No, don't think so. Local call.'

Max leaned across the table and took the cigarette from her fingers. He placed it on the saucer and cupped his right hand under her chin. 'I'm deaf, Miss Crown, but I can lip-read. However, you mumble. Plus you cover your mouth with your fucking cigarette and your face with your hair. I'm going to ask you a couple of questions and you're going to forget about smoking, speak clearly and answer them truthfully. Otherwise, everything we know about this place will be loaded onto you. Understand?'

Both gesture and statement were very forceful and threatening and Eve Crown was in a vulnerable condition. Tears sprung into her eyes and she nodded. She reached for the cigarette, remembered, and let it lie smouldering. The smoke drifted up into her face and there was misery and despair in every line and wrinkle. She tried to suck in a deep breath but it caught and became a gasping wheeze. Her voice was a cracked ruin. 'Yes,' she whispered.

'Do you know where Andrea got her money from?'

'She told people she inherited it, but she told *me* it was pay-off money for something that had happened when she was a cop. This . . . this was when we were in love and didn't have secrets from each other.'

'OK,' Max said. 'Over the eight years you lived together, did she ever go anywhere regularly, get letters or phone calls from anywhere frequently? Some important place?'

This was as long as Eve Crown could bear to go without filling her lungs with tobacco smoke. She picked up the cigarette, took a deep drag and butted it. She lifted her head and expelled the smoke in a long plume over Max's head. 'What did that dickhead American President say? Read my lips? Well, read my fucking lips. She got letters and phone calls from the Gold Coast and she went up there a bit. And you can bet your two rotten, stinking dicks and your four rotten, stinking balls that's where she's gone now!'

'I wonder,' Max said as we left the gallery, 'if the quit smoking people used a slogan like "It takes years off your life and puts years on your face", women would give it up? She'd be good-looking if she hadn't ruined herself by smoking.'

Max clearly had women on his mind. I hadn't noticed the potential in Eve Crown, but then I had actual beauty to deal with in Claudia. 'It'd sound better round the other way,' I said. 'But, no, I reckon people smoke because they want to or have to. Something has to change fundamentally to get them off it.'

'Suppose you're right. I never took it up. You?'

'Stopped years ago.'

'What changed fundamentally?'

'I forget. Pretty obvious isn't it, Max? Someone tipped Andrea off that we were coming.'

'Right. Let's talk about that.' He headed towards the oval and we found seats that looked out over the greenery. 'Nice spot this, quiet. It gets tiring coping with all the mishmash of noise. I take it you haven't discussed the case with anyone, so the problem has to be at my end. Someone in the works is keeping an eye on me.'

I nodded. I'd told Claudia about the case in some detail but I certainly hadn't mentioned Andrea Neville, aka Craig. 'Keeping an eye on *us*,' I said. 'I got worked over after leaving the Beckett house yesterday.'

I told Max about the oddly restrained beating and its aftermath. He raised his eyebrows. 'I never heard of anything like that before.'

'It's weird. Suppose someone's trying to stop us finding out who killed Ramona. He bumps Barry White but he just warns me and Andrea Craig. It doesn't make sense.'

Max plucked up a stalk of grass and started splitting it with his thumbnail. 'Thank Christ I haven't made any noises about Peggy Hawkins or Colin Sligo. It looks as if I'll have to go to other sources to make inquiries about them.'

'We'd better get up there,' I said. 'I've got some contacts. That'll just about run out Barry's retainer. This is going to cost me money.'

'Any luck at the Connaught?'

For a moment I didn't get his meaning, then I did. *All the luck in the world*, I thought, but it wasn't the time for explanations so I shook my head. Then another thought hit me. 'Leo Grogan,' I said. 'I wonder if Leo's all right.'

I found Grogan's number in my notebook. We went back to the car and I rang it and asked for him. The woman who answered the phone told me that Mr Grogan was in hospital. He'd had a very bad fall down some steep steps. His skull was fractured and he had internal injuries. She didn't sound as if she was too keen on Leo, and there was something very like satisfaction in her voice when she added, 'He's not expected to live.'

I relayed this to Max. 'I'm worried about Penny,' he said. 'Ring her, will you?'

I rang, got her on the line and handed the phone to Max. 'Penny, I want you to drop anything you might be working on for me and seal it up tight. Don't do another thing. OK?'

This time I was the relayer. 'She says it's not OK, that you shouldn't patronise her and she asks what's up.'

Max took the phone. 'Take some of that leave you're due. Go to your sister's place and stay there until you hear from me.'

I regained the phone and listened. 'She says get stuffed,' I said. 'She says she'll work on what she pleases and she knows how to keep it secure. She says she's got a gun and she knows how to use it.'

'Shit,' Max said.

'He says "shit",' I said to Penny.

'I heard him,' Penny said. 'Tell him to take care of himself and not to worry about me. Goodbye.'

'She hung up on us, Max. She says you should take care of yourself and not worry about her.' Turning to face him every time I had to speak was giving me a crick in the neck. I probably looked pained.

Max noticed of course and he grinned at me. 'It's a bastard working with the disabled, isn't it? They're so fucking stubborn and it takes just that much more effort. I sometimes get that way with Penny and she gets the same with me. It's lots of fun.'

It was late in the morning and the interior of the car was hot. My torn ear was throbbing and my battered ribs were aching. I wanted to be between Claudia's silk sheets and feel her cool hands on my body. Max was right. I felt irritated by his deafness and guilty about feeling like that. 'I need a drink and some pain-killers,' I said. 'I suggest we find a pub and make a plan.'

'You don't think it's worthwhile looking in on Leo Grogan?'

I was thinking ahead, selfishly. Thinking about an afternoon with Claudia before a flight to the Gold Coast. Everything heals up faster in a warm climate. 'I don't, and the chances are that whoever tried to kill him would be looking out for us. Why make it easy?'

Max nodded. 'A beer and a ploughman's lunch'd go down well.'

Half an hour later we were sitting in an Oxford Street pub with two middies and plates of cheese, bread and pickled onions. I had three Panadols inside me and was feeling less pain. I'd rung Qantas and booked us on a 6.30 p.m. flight to Coolangatta, loading up the American Express card. Max waited until the video clip on the giant TV at the end of the bar finished blasting and he'd swallowed a lump of bread and cheese before speaking.

'My guess is that it's Sligo. He's got someone down here checking on things that might jump up and grab him. When I got appointed he'd have heard of it and taken steps. He was as crooked as they come, and the Beckett thing was probably only one of his earners.'

I drank some beer and nibbled on the cheese. Opening my mouth wide enough to get my teeth into the bread hurt. 'Could be. Trouble is, if he's monitoring the whole thing he might've done something about Peggy Hawkins.'

Max crunched a pickled onion enthusiastically. Presumably he didn't have to worry about the state of his breath through the afternoon. 'From what I've heard of Peggy,' he said, 'she'd make dirty old Colin look like a boy scout.'

We agreed to meet at the Qantas terminal at five-thirty.

I phoned Claudia and got her answering machine. Somehow I'd expected her to be there but there

132

was no reason she should be. It looked as if my chances of a soothing afternoon were slim. Disappointed, I drove back to Glebe. I decided that Bob Lowenstein was the man to help me on the Gold Coast, but my mind kept flicking back to Claudia. I turned into my street and saw the green Laser parked outside the house. I could feel the smile forming on my face as I pulled up behind it. She was at the front door, just straightening up. There's something very pleasing about the shape of a woman's behind in that position, especially when it's enclosed in a tight skirt.

I got out of the car quietly and stood at the front gate. She straightened up, turned around and saw me.

'Wanna buy a house, lady?' I said.

'Oh god, I've just written you a note.'

I flipped open the letterbox. 'Good, there's nothing here worth reading.'

She came down the path. 'You'll think I'm pushy.'

'Push all you like. I phoned, you went one better.'

I opened the gate and reached for her. She put her arms around me and the pain made me gasp, drop my keys and clutch at the fence.

'Cliff, what's the matter? What's happened to you?'

'Tell you inside. Will you pick up the keys, please. I can't bend.'

She pampered me, made me coffee, gave me a sponge bath and packed my overnight bag for

133

me. I told her where I was going and, in a general way, why. She said I should be careful and that she wished she could go with me and I said next time for sure. Ian Sangster was right, the missionary position wasn't on, but there are other ways.

15

Bob Lowenstein runs a private detective agency in Broadbeach, close to Surfers Paradise. He used to work in Sydney until an arthritic hip got so bad he had to move to a warmer climate. I advised him to have a hip replacement and stay in civilisation, but he was a Christian Scientist of sorts and didn't believe in arthritis or surgery. He went north, tried natural remedies and hydrotherapy and the hip got a bit better, thus proving, to him, that modern medicine was all gimcrackery and that Mary Baker Eddy had it right all along. Despite this, he was an intelligent and amusing guy who had taken to the computer like a plumber to PVC. He made a good living running credit checks on people for the hotels and the casino, locating missing kids courtesy of the CES computer and checking insurance claims. Lots of dodgy insurance claims on the Gold Coast. Bob was one of the very few people I corresponded with. His letters came to me immaculately from the word processor and I scrawled a few lines on postcards in reply. He'd bought a small apartment block and had often invited me to come and stay.

I rang him from the airport while Max arranged the car hire.

'Bob, Cliff Hardy, how's the other hip?'

'Both hips doing fine, no thanks to you. Where are you?'

'Almost on your doorstep. Can you put me and a mate up for a few days? We sort of don't need to sign hotel registers or use credit cards. Might need a bit of help from your computer as well. You can bill me.'

'Sure, got a flat vacant. Be glad to see you, Cliff. Bill your client, don't you mean?'

'Thereby hangs a tale. We'll be along soon, Bob. And thanks.'

The air carried just a touch of that tropical tang as we walked through the car park to pick up the Laser Max had hired while I was talking to Bob. *Good choice*, I thought. I wore my old linen jacket, a denim shirt and newish jeans. Max was in the mood with cotton slacks and a Hawaiian shirt.

'It's a funny thing,' he said as we got into the car. 'But the traffic authority doesn't seem to think hearing is relevant to driving. No endorsement on the licence. I nearly had a half a dozen prangs before I got used to looking hard and really reading the traffic.'

'I'm glad of that,' I said. 'Because this is a manual with a floor shift and driving it would be tricky for me with these ribs. You're in charge, mate. We're going to the Florida Apartments in Broadbeach.'

Max reached into the glove compartment,

136

consulted the local street directory briefly and started the car. Normally, I'm a nervous passenger, but he drove extremely well, decisively with good judgment. I relaxed and told him a bit about Bob Lowenstein as I looked out on the sun-faded strip development of used-car lots and fast-food joints with the Surfers Paradise high-rise in the distance.

'Sounds like a good man. A Christian Scientist, eh? They must be a dying breed. What're you, Cliff?'

'A pagan.'

Max overtook a Kombi van with a roof-rack that held at least three surfboards and cruised up behind a white BMW. He shot a quick glance sideways to get my reply. 'Me, too,' he said. 'Me, too.'

The Florida Apartments was a white stucco block comprising four self-contained flats just back from the highway. No view of the water, good view of the casino. Bob Lowenstein had lost hair and gained weight since shifting to Queensland, but I have to admit that he was moving better. He shook our hands, admired Max's shirt, settled us into the vacant flat, phoned for a pizza and opened two bottles of red wine.

'Tell me, tell me,' he said. 'I'm fucking dying to hear what you big-city detectives are up to these days.'

We were sitting in Bob's downstairs flat, the biggest of the four. Ours was directly above. Bob's housekeeping was basic; we ate the pizza straight from the box and he produced a toilet roll for us to wipe our hands on. The wine we drank from the kind of glasses you can bounce on a cement slab. It was good wine, though. I gave him the gist over a couple of glasses and answered his questions in between slices of pizza. Bob had grown a thick moustache to compensate for the loss on top and this made it difficult for Max to lip-read him. I could feel his irritation and didn't blame him for getting stuck solidly into the red.

'I wouldn't give shit for your chances,' Bob said when I wound up.

'Thanks, Bob. Wouldn't you say a million bucks is worth playing a long shot?'

Bob shook his head. 'The bloody lawyer'll chisel you out of it somehow even if you do get a sniff. Sounds to me like the lawyer put the heavies onto you.'

I recalled Cavendish on the mobile as I left the Beckett house. 'Maybe.' I turned to face Max who was pouring himself another glass. 'Bob does this, knocks everything on the head then hops in and shows you how it should be done.'

'Good,' Max said. 'Let's see you hop, Bob.'

Bob wiped his hands and his moustache, slid the few bits of crust and droppings into the box and dumped it into a bin in the kitchen. He came back with a notebook computer and another bottle. I looked at Max and he shook his head.

'Coffee, Bob.'

'Pikers, it's on. This is for me.' He turned the computer on and started tapping. 'Right, now, first up, Colin fucking Sligo. I take it you want dirt on him? Some leverage?'

'Wouldn't hurt. And his current circumstances, how he stands with the powers-that-be, retirement date, health, you know.'

'I know, I know,' Bob said. 'Plus you need an address and info on Peggy Hawkins. Shouldn't be too hard. What's her line, bowls, golf, gambling, booze . . . ?'

'Sex,' I said. 'Our information is that she's most likely to be working in the sex industry, in one capacity or another.'

'You didn't tell me that,' Max said.

'You never asked.'

'Easy, that should be.' Bob said. 'Now about Andrea Craig. Is she likely to link up with Peggy?'

'They were both screwing Johnno Hawkins. Who knows?'

Bob tapped the keys. 'Hawkins, Craig, Neville . . . ages, any descriptions?'

'Not sure,' I said. 'Peggy could be forty plus, Andrea a bit younger, maybe. Peggy was thin and dark with big tits fifteen years ago.'

Bob's balding head was bent over the keyboard. He made a Roy Orbison growl. 'Sounds good but women change.'

'Yeah.' Tired and a bit drunk, I tried to recall the trashed photograph. 'Neville or Craig is or was blonde. Big eyes.'

'Lesbian,' Max said. 'Very small mouth.'

'No disadvantage,' Bob said.

Max had adjusted to the moustache and was following. We were three men without women, all a bit pissed. We all laughed.

There was no food in our flat so in the morning Max and I went down to Bob's. We found him reading the paper and eating crumpets with honey, accounting for the expanding waistline.

'No challenge,' Bob said when we appeared. 'Or not much of a one.'

I put the rest of last night's coffee on to reheat and dropped four slices into the toaster. Max looked seedy. 'How's that?' I said.

'You'll like this. Peg Hawkins runs a brothel in Surfers by the name of Satisfaction. High-class place apparently. She lives on the premises and runs a tight ship. In good standing with the council and with the constabulary and—wait for it men—one senior member in particular.'

'No,' I said. The toast popped and the coffee got hot.

'That's right. Deputy Commissioner Sligo is a devoted customer. Word is, Peg services him personally. I got this from a journo of absolute unreliability, mind. Needed confirmation and I got it. Silly fucker uses his credit card but not, I'm happy to say, his departmental one.'

I poured two mugs of coffee, buttered the toast and brought the lot over to the table where Max sat with his head in his hands. 'I should never drink red wine,' he said.

'Balls,' Bob said. 'It's good for your heart.'

Max groaned. 'It's my head I'm worried about. Got any pain-killers?'

'Panadol. Top drawer. Col's pretty dirty by all accounts, but he's got less than a year to run on his contract and the general view is that everyone's happy to let him go quietly.'

I got the Panadol from the drawer and put the packet in front of Max. 'That's useful, Bob. He might be open to some persuasion.'

'Yup. He doesn't do much these days. Plays a lot of golf at Robina. Easy to get a quiet word with him. I've got the licence photos of all three for you. Col's the ugliest, needless to say. Peg still looks pretty well-preserved. Can't tell about the tits of course. Craig was booked for speeding yesterday in Kempsey. Driving a yellow Subaru coupe. I've got the registration number. Going north obviously, but whether she's come up here or not I can't say until she buys something with a credit card, checks into a hotel or breaks the fucking law.'

I looked at Max who had taken a couple of capsules with his coffee and was nibbling on a piece of toast. 'This is the sort of thing that's putting blokes like me out of business.'

'Dinosaurs,' Bob said. 'D'you want to know when Sligo's teeing off next at Robina?'

'Come on,' I said.

'I kid you not. They put the tee-off times on the computer and the computer's hooked to a modem. If you know the password to the system you're in like Flynn.'

'Passwords are secret by definition.'

'Hah,' Bob said. 'They're a tradeable commodity, like everything else. I know bloody hundreds and I can trade with the best of them.'

I drank some coffee and ate some toast. I'd managed to sleep on the undamaged ear and the ribs weren't hurting much. And I was more practised at drinking red wine than Max. I felt pretty good and optimistic, although I was still worried that finding out who'd paid off Hawkins might not lead any further. 'I'm impressed,' I said.

'You should be,' Bob said smugly. 'Colin tees off at eleven this very day. They're playing a four-person Ambrose, whatever that is. Apparently they take a rest after the first nine holes. That'll be around twelve-thirty.'

'Where's Robina?' I said.

Bob pointed out of the window. 'Just down the way.'

I turned to Max who was looking better by the minute. He tackled a second piece of toast. 'You getting all this, Max?'

'Enough.'

'Would you rather tackle Peggy or Colin? I'm easy.'

'I think the fresh air'd do me good.'

'OK.'

'I wish we could round up Craig,' Max said. 'She could be very useful to use against one or both of them.'

Bob ripped off a metre of toilet paper and wiped his fingers. 'You don't know anything about her Queensland connections?'

'Just that she made a lot of phone calls to the Gold Coast,' Max said.

'Shit, why didn't you tell me that? What number did she call from?'

Max consulted his notebook and gave Bob the number of the gallery. 'Leave it with me,' Bob said. 'I'll be able to give you the Queensland contact in a couple of hours. I gotta admit it, this is more fun than repossessing cars.'

I thought about Max's concern for Penny Draper and realised that we'd told Bob almost everything there was to know and, unlike my sketchy account to Claudia, we'd included names and details. Bob had never been a man of action and as I looked at him now, balding and soft around the middle, a key-tapper, I felt guilty.

'Look, Bob,' I said. 'Somebody bumped Barry White and had a good go at Leo Grogan. Somebody's playing for keeps in this thing and we don't have a clue who it is. He or they seem to have been keeping tabs on me and might know we're here.'

'So?' Bob said.

'So you should be careful.'

Bob smiled. 'Fuck you, Cliff. You think this computer work is cosy and safe. Two weeks ago a guy took a sledge to that front door there and wanted to do the same thing to my head.'

'What happened?'

'I shot the fucker,' Bob said.

16

We took a swim in the apartment block pool which was barely long enough to get a few decent strokes in, but helped to start the day fresh. I'd taken off the rib-wrapping and confined myself to a gentle breaststroke. The aches and bruises were fading. Max surprised me; he had a powerful stroke that cut neatly through the water. He was carrying some flesh around his waist like me but was in pretty good shape for a man pushing sixty. He kept at it longer than I did and looked as if he could have done a good bit more.

'That was good,' he said when he flopped out of the pool. I'd come carefully up the metal ladder. 'Good antidote to the wine. Think I'll stick to beer.'

'Nothing wrong with Fourex,' I said. 'You're happy about taking Sligo on your own?'

'It'll be a pleasure.'

I'd towelled off and was stretched out on the tiles enjoying the morning sun. 'If Sligo's the one keeping an eye on things in Sydney he could have some pretty handy help up here.'

Max had brought a small toilet bag down with

him. He dried his hair and shook water from his ears. Then he cleaned them with a cotton bud before putting in the hearing aids. The hangover frown had lifted and when he slicked back his hair with a comb he looked younger and more lively than I'd seen him before. 'I've been thinking about that,' he said. 'I've changed my mind. I reckon these Queenslanders are bit players in all this. Important for the information they might have, but ... remittance men and women as it were, if you see what I mean. Sligo included. The real energy's in Sydney.'

'Cavendish and whoever suppressed the note?'

'I think so.'

'But that someone has a handle on what you've been doing.'

'Or on what *you've* been doing, Cliff. Think about how Bob can sneak into things. You use a mobile phone, and a fax machine, don't you?'

'Yeah, but ...'

Max shifted as a ray of sunlight hit us, dazzled him, and prevented him from seeing what I was saying.

'What's that?'

'Nothing,' I said. 'It's confusing the way it always is for me.'

'Good. You're in familiar territory. I've had a word with Bob. He's got some more information and some good ideas. I think you should listen to him.'

I was conscious that I didn't have any very good ideas myself about how to question Peg

Hawkins and Sligo beyond a vague notion of divide and rule. Bob was busy at his computer in a room off the kitchen. He shook one fist in the air while the other hand still worked at the keyboard.

'What?' I said.

'Your Andrea Craig not infrequently called Peg Hawkins' unlisted number.'

'You're amazing, Bob.'

'I know, I know. Look, I've dug up a couple of mobiles for you blokes to use.'

'Max can't use a phone.'

'That's why I'm going with him. One of the reasons. The other is to see Colin Sligo eating shit. Now this is what I reckon you should do.'

Bob and Max set off in the Laser for Robina and I got a cab to The Esplanade where Satisfaction was located, along with Satin & Silk, Fun Girls and Good for You. It was a little early to go calling on a lady of the night but that can be the best time to catch one, before the hard shell slides into place and time becomes money in the most direct way. Prostitution is illegal in Queensland, but the authorities seemed to be turning a blind eye. Like any well-conducted brothel, Satisfaction put a couple of barriers up between it and people on the street. A small garden in front of the two-storey, white-painted building was screened off by latticework and when you were behind that you still had a security grille to get through before you got to the front door.

It was cool and shady in the garden with a

strong scent of jasmine. I pushed the buzzer on the grille and got a recorded message: 'This is Satisfaction, an escort service and relaxation centre. If you wish to enter please press the buzzer twice.' Then the message was repeated in what sounded like Japanese.

I pressed and the grille slid open. The front door opened as I approached and a slender blonde woman wearing a black lace wrap over a red silk teddy and red very high heels looked me up and down.

'Good morning, sir,' she said. 'Can I help you?'

'Yes, I'd like to spend some time with one of your ladies.'

'Of course. Please come in. I'm Amanda. As you see, I'm a blonde, but if you'd prefer a brunette or a redhead I'm sure Chantelle or . . .'

I kept moving past her and along the hall towards a huge mirror that noticeably slimmed me down. Amanda came after me, still chanting her spiel, swaying on the heels, maybe already sensing that something was wrong. She reached out, took my arm and tried to draw me towards her and her headily perfumed body that gave off only a slight tang of cigarette smoke and musk oil.

'If you'd like to wait in there, sir, on the left, we can talk a little more. I'm afraid you can't just walk about. Our guests want privacy as I'm sure you do . . .'

Not breaking her hold and taking her other arm in a soft grip, I let her steer me into a small room which contained a bar, a couch and a TV set with a video playing. Two women, one black and one white, were to-and-fro'ing on a bed, sharing a deeply-inserted double dildo and out-doing each other with their low moans.

'Do you like that?' Amanda said.

'Not quite my scene. I want to see Peg Hawkins.'

'I'm afraid . . .'

'There's nothing to be afraid of,' I said. 'Just tell her I'm a friend of Colin Sligo. You might mention that I knew Johnno pretty well and I also know Andrea Craig. Have you got all that?'

She broke free and all the softness and lubri-ciousness went out of her. 'A copper, are you?'

'Worse, Amanda, something much worse. And tell Peg not to try and duck out because I've got some people outside you ladies really wouldn't want to meet. You really wouldn't.'

'We've got protection here.'

'Look, if Peg's in this room inside five minutes you won't need protection or anything like it. We talk, I go. If she's not, I guarantee you'll be looking for another position and the word'll be out on you and it won't be easy to get something else this good. Now, be sensible.'

'What name'll I say?'

I looked at her and shook my head.

'OK, I'll fetch her. Stay here, will you? There's a fat Jap getting a blow job next door. If he sees you he'll freak.'

'Three minutes,' I said.

Peg was down in less than that. She wore a white

linen sleeveless dress with a pleated front and skirt. She showed just enough cleavage to indicate how impressive the rest of her would be. She was still thin, about medium height in medium heels and her lightly tanned skin, blonde streaked hair and make-up were all designed to make her look cool, successful and no older than she had to. It worked. Peg Hawkins must have been well over forty and must have had some hard years, but they weren't showing yet. She came into the room and more or less ignored me while she turned off the television and told Amanda to keep an eye on things.

'Now,' she said. 'Having succeeded in frightening young Amanda you can try me. I'll return the compliment. I'll give you five minutes and if you haven't accounted for yourself by then you'll be wishing you had.'

'I don't want to frighten you, Peg.' I took out my PEA licence and showed it to her. 'I want to talk about Ramona Beckett, Johnno your late hubby, Colin Sligo, Amanda Neville or Craig— people like that.'

She'd been standing up, rather stagily, beside the TV and her face had worn a look of indifference. But the names hit her hard. She moved sideways and sat on the couch. Her mouth twitched and a few cracks appeared in the flawless make-up around her eyes.

'Jesus,' she said. 'After all this time.'

'It has been a while,' I said.

'Yeah. Make me a drink, will you? Vodka and tonic.'

I went to the bar, mixed Smirnoff and lo-cal tonic water, added some ice cubes and handed it to her. I settled for the tonic and ice myself. She took a slug and settled back against the couch. Her hands, clutched around the glass, looked a little older than the rest of her.

'Are you still getting a pay-off, Peg?'

She nodded.

'And Johnno's super?'

Another nod.

'The super doesn't have to stop and the Taxation Department doesn't need to know about the other money. You don't have to be charged with conspiracy to commit murder, money-laundering and all the other stuff. Not if you don't want to be.'

'You could be bluffing.'

I drank, rattled the ice cubes. 'A colleague of mine is out at Robina talking to Colin right now. We know that Amanda Craig is on her way up here. Maybe she rang you from Kempsey after she got booked for speeding.'

'Stupid bitch!'

'An ex-cop named Barry White is dead and another named Leo Grogan's in intensive care.' I turned to show her my stitched ear. 'I got a bit of a hammering myself. It's all breaking open, Peg, and people are going to suffer. You could be one of them.'

'I don't know anything about dead coppers.'

'Maybe I believe you. Whether I do or don't won't matter if you tell me what I really want to know.'

150

She sucked in a deep breath and the large breasts rose and fell eye-catchingly. She must have used the movement many times for her own ends but she wasn't doing anything like that now. She was just taking in oxygen, just buying time. 'And what the fuck's that?'

'Who paid Johnno and Sligo and Andrea to suppress the kidnapping note after Ramona Beckett went missing?'

17

Peg Hawkins bit her lip and got lipstick on her beautifully capped teeth. Her fingernails were long and painted a muted shade of red. She tapped them against the glass, then picked at them and some flakes of paint fell off. Any minute now she'd put her hand up to her hair and disturb the carefully sprayed arrangement. I didn't want to see it. She was a handsome, well-presented women, and I didn't get any pleasure from seeing her come apart.

'Come on, Peg,' I said. 'A name and a few details and it'll be done.'

'It's not that easy.'

'Maybe not, but you haven't got much option. Fact is, I've got bigger fish to fry. This looks like a nice establishment. You're doing well, providing an essential service. All fine by me and my colleague. Why put it at risk?'

She chewed at her lip and the colour spread on her teeth, threatening to make her look clownish. I got out a tissue and handed it to her. 'You're messing yourself up.'

She stood and looked at herself in the mirror

above the TV set. 'Jesus,' she said. 'You're turning me into a hag.' She made repairs and straightened herself up. She threw out her chest and this time she was working at it. 'Look, whatever your name is, as you say, this is a classy place. I've got some very talented women here. Is there some other way we can work it out?'

I shook my head. 'I can't quite see what your problem is, Peg. But, no. No chance of anything like that.'

'Didn't think so. A tough bastard, like Johnno. What's your name again?'

'Cliff Hardy.'

She sighed and held out her glass to me. She was still working. The long, slender, tanned arm came out like an invitation. 'Normally, I don't drink till six, Cliff.'

'Me too. Normally.' I made her another drink and topped up mine.

'The problem is Colin,' she said.

It felt like the right moment. I got the mobile from my jacket pocket and punched in the numbers. I switched it to Broadcast so Peg could hear the exchange.

'This is Bob.'

'Cliff, Bob. Has Max talked to Sligo?'

'Happening now. He had a good first nine but I don't think he's going to putt so well on the back nine. See, I'm picking up the language.'

'Have we got the name?'

'Yeah,' Bob said. 'It's who you thought. Colin says Johnno got all the cream. He says Peg's a great root but not very bright. He's still talking.'

'That fucking bastard!' Peg threw her glass at the TV set. It bounced off and broke. 'He got just as much from Beckett as Johnno, maybe more.'

'Thanks, Bob.' I cut the connection. 'That'd be Sean Beckett?'

'Yeah, of course.'

'How would Sligo get more out of him?'

'He claimed to know who the kidnappers were, even though he didn't have a fucking clue.'

The door opened and Amanda, looking agitated, took a tentative step into the room.

'It's all right, Mandy,' Peg said. 'I just lost my block for a minute. Nothing to worry about.'

Amanda barely looked at the broken glass on the floor. 'It's not that, Peggy. There's a woman here insisting on seeing you. I really don't know how to cope with this sort of . . .'

The door swung wide and another woman came into the room. Unlike the other two, there was nothing sexually alluring about her. She wore jeans, boots and a sweater. No make-up. Her hair was short and straight, her eyes were big and her mouth was small.

'Hullo, Andrea,' I said. I ushered Amanda out quickly and shut the door.

'Who the fuck's this?' Andrea Craig said.

I held up the mobile phone. 'You left a very unhappy woman behind you. Want me to give Eve a ring and tell her you're OK?'

Andrea looked at Peg as if she wanted to do her serious harm. 'What have you been doing, you dumb bitch? What's going wrong?'

Peg shrugged, went to the bar and made

herself another drink. 'Colin's spilled the beans.'

'Colin? I don't believe it.'

Peg had a drink, then poured in more vodka. 'Ask him. He seems to know everything about everybody.'

'That's right, you slut. Get pissed and slide out of it. I suppose you're fucking this hard case?'

'I bet he'd rather fuck me than you. You look like shit. At least when you were rooting Johnno you looked like a woman.'

'All you know about being a woman is how to open your legs.'

'That's enough!' I said. 'I know you got a phone call and came running to see Peg. I want to know why and who tipped you off.'

Andrea pulled a packet of cigarettes and a lighter from her jeans pocket. 'Get fucked!'

Peg took two steps towards her and knocked the cigarettes and lighter to the floor. The packet fell open and the cigarettes spilled out onto the wet carpet. Andrea yelped.

'Nobody smokes in here,' Peg said. 'Not you, not Colin, not the fucking Bishop of Brisbane. You'd better talk to this bloke. He's got Colin by the balls somehow and the whole thing's turning to shit. I'll tell you this, Hardy. This bitch put the screws on Johnno. She claimed to have something that proved he'd done some big favour for Sean Beckett.'

'You bet I have,' Andrea said.

I said, 'What?'

Andrea looked weary. The adrenalin that had carried her from Sydney to the Gold Coast was fading and she looked ready to drop her bundle. 'Why should I tell you?' she muttered. 'You wouldn't know shit about it.'

'I know there was a ransom note that got suppressed.'

She stared at me, fumbled for her cigarettes, remembered and twitched visibly. 'Yeah, well I've got that fucking note. I need a smoke.'

'You can smoke all you like in a couple of minutes. Two more questions. Why did you call Peggy and visit here so much? It's clear you can't stand each other.'

'I'll answer that,' Peg said. 'It was Johnno's doing. He stashed away a hell of a lot of money in an account up here. A lawyer makes periodical withdrawals and deposits it in another account. We can only draw on it jointly with both signatures.'

'I don't get it,' I said. 'Why?'

'Because he was a sadistic bastard. This was his way of punishing both of us. Her for black-mailing him, me because I wouldn't give him the show he wanted.'

'Shut up,' Andrea spat.

'Fuck you! He might as well know it all. When he ran out of poke on account of booze and diabetes, Johnno liked to watch two women perform. It would've given him the thrill of a lifetime to see his wife and his mistress sucking each other. This dyke slut was more than willing but I wasn't.'

'It'd be a dry twat now,' Andrea said. 'Probably got a few stitches in it to draw it closed.'

'This is unedifying,' I said. 'What's the lawyer's name?'

'I thought you knew everything,' Peg said. 'Looks like you don't.'

'Cavendish,' I said. 'Wallace Cavendish.'

'Jesus,' Andrea said. 'How the fuck did all this get out in the open? I thought it was sealed up tight. Johnno couldn't have been as fucking smart as he thought he was.'

I had a sense that the women, despite their loathing for each other, might suddenly team up and put me out of the game. I was trying to think fast enough to ask the right questions while I still had them, but there were a lot of pieces to put together. Andrea moved to the bar, pulled out an ice-cube tray, twisted it and let three cubes drop in a glass. The rest fell on the floor. She poured a couple of fingers of Teachers into the glass and took a drink. She bent down and picked up a couple of cigarettes and examined them for useability.

Just then the mobile rang. I answered and forgot that I still had it on Broadcast.

'Cliff,' Bob announced for all to hear. 'I hope it worked because we can't hang around here much longer. Sligo never showed up. He called in sick. What . . .'

Peg Hawkins swore and came at me with her fingernails hooked like talons. But she'd taken in too much vodka, too early in the day, too quickly. She slashed but missed, lost balance and fell heavily. Andrea laughed and kicked her in the ribs with a heavy boot.

157

'Who's dumb now, bitch?' she said. 'He fucking fooled you, didn't he? I knew Colin'd never spill his guts.' She landed another kick. Peg rolled away, right into the broken glass. A long shard bit into her upper arm and the blood ran, staining the white dress. Andrea laughed again and headed for the door.

I missed a beat, still holding the squawking mobile, looking at the hard-shelled, elegant woman reduced to a weeping wreck on the soggy carpet. I cut the connection and moved out into the passage. Amanda tried to block Andrea's way but the ex-policewoman had too many moves for her and Amanda ended up on the floor. But Andrea had to press a bell to open the door and that gave me time to catch her. I went through the door with a strong grip on her arm as a counter to her attempt to twist me sideways and get a well applied boot to my shins.

We were locked together, sweating and panting in the perfumed garden. I pressed her up against the trellis with a forearm under her chin and a knee in her groin. My bruised ribs were shrieking and I knew I couldn't hold her there for long.

Our faces were close together and the sour, tobacco odour of her breath was strong in my nostrils.

'One answer to one question, Andrea, and you can walk away from all this.'

'What's that, arsehole?'

'Who tipped you off in Sydney? Who sent you running up here to Peg and the money?'

'That's two fucking questions and I don't know the fucking answers.'

'You got a phone call. Eve told us.'

I felt the strength go out of her but I held on tight in case she was faking. 'Eve,' she said. 'Poor old Eve.'

'Who?'

'I don't know. Some woman.'

'A woman?'

'That's right. Another surprise for you is it, arsehole? You think only men can fuck people around?'

'No,' I said. 'I don't think that.'

'Bet your arse. This woman said the Ramona Beckett thing was being investigated and that my name had come up. She said these hard types . . . ease up, you're fucking choking me.'

I relaxed the pressure, a little.

'. . . were coming to see me and I'd better get out of it and grab everything I could lay my hands on before it all turned to shit. Let go!'

I released her, she spat in my face and ran away. I leaned back against the trellis, wiped my face with the back of my hand and closed my eyes for a second. When I opened them Peg Hawkins was standing by the open grille. She had a white handtowel pressed against her cut arm and the blood was just beginning to seep through it. Her dress was stained and spotted. She was pale but she was fighting for control.

'What now?' she said.

I shook my head and stood straight, looking

back at her. 'Do you know who killed Ramona Beckett?'

'I don't know and I don't care.'

'Why did Beckett go on paying after Johnno died? Why wasn't he off the hook then?'

'Johnno was a sadistic, twisted creep, but he was smart. He had Beckett on tape.'

'Where's the tape now?'

'Wouldn't you like to know!'

'Yeah, I would, but I do know something. Peg. I reckon that money's going to stop coming.'

'Why?'

I reached into my jacket pocket and took out the miniature tape recorder I'd activated just before I'd pressed the Satisfaction buzzer. The red light was showing and the tape was still running.

'I've got a tape of my own,' I said. 'Does that make me smart, too?'

'What're you going to do with it?'

'Play it to Colin Sligo for one thing.'

She sagged against the grille. 'Oh, Jesus,' she said. 'Don't do that. Please don't do that. I can get along without the money from Sydney, but Colin can put me out of business here.'

'You'd better get that arm looked at. I'll do a deal with you, Peg. I won't play the tape to Sligo—or only an edited version. I'll do everything I can to keep you out of it.'

'What do I have to do in return?'

'One, don't contact Sligo today. Two, tell me where Andrea Craig's likely to have gone.'

Peggy Hawkins was a woman of spirit. Despite her distress and her wound she managed

160

a harsh, genuine laugh. 'Fuck me,' she said. 'I'll have to trust you.'

'That's right.'

'Sure I can't interest you in Amanda or Chantelle? I can scrub up pretty well myself too.'

'I don't doubt it, but no.'

'Not queer, are you, Cliff?'

'What do you think?'

She sighed. The breasts heaved. She was almost back in business. 'No, I understand men better than anything else. I've watched you. You're a hair, eyes, mouth, tit and leg man. Johnno was much the same before he got old and fat. Don't get old and fat, Cliff.'

'I'll be careful about fat.'

'You've got a deal. In fact I think I'll take myself off somewhere for a while.'

'Good idea.'

'Andrea's got a girlfriend in Byron Bay. Name of Jackie. She's a hooker who works out of a duplex opposite the main beach. I think her name might be Jackson, I'm not sure. Anyway, that's the name she uses. Things should be quiet there about now. I don't know the address, but Andrea doesn't know that I know.'

'Thanks, Peg.'

She pressed the buzzer and the message began: 'This is Satisfaction, an escort service and . . .'

18

I used the mobile to call Bob and Max who were heading back towards Broadbeach.

'How'd it go?' Bob said. 'Hope I didn't call back too soon.'

'No, the timing was about right. It worked pretty well. I think we've got what we need. A couple of loose ends. I need a drink, mate. I can see something called the Honolulu Bar dead ahead. That's where I'll be.'

'You all right?'

'Yeah, fine. It's lucky I like beating up women.'

I was on my second vodka and tonic (the first was a silent toast to Peggy Hawkins and after that I couldn't see any reason to change drinks), when Max and Bob came into the bar. It wasn't quite as bad as it sounded—there was less bamboo than you'd expect, fewer fake leis, and only one poster of Elvis as he appeared in *Blue Hawaii*.

They took stools on either side of me. Bob ordered a beer and Max a mineral water with lemon. I downed my drink and ordered another.

'This is no good,' I said. 'I'll have to swivel my head so Max can see what I'm saying.'

'What's wrong with you?' Bob said. 'You're on the way to getting pissed. I thought you said everything went well?'

We moved to a table overlooking the street and not far from Satisfaction. I was beginning to tell them what had happened when Peggy Hawkins came from behind the trellis and got into a taxi. She was wearing a tight blue dress and a black jacket and I saw the driver miss his grip on the door after she slid inside.

I lifted my glass. 'Cheers, Peg.'

'He's flipped,' Bob said. 'Must be the climate.'

I played the tape for them, stopping and starting, repeating certain sections until they had the whole picture. They said nothing until Max drained his second mineral water. 'I think I'll have a beer. What about you?'

Bob and I ordered and when Max came back with the drinks he said, 'I feel like Bogart in *Casablanca*. Play it again, Cliff.'

I knew what he meant. I'd made a mental note of the counter on the tape at the spot. I ran through to it and hit the button. First my voice, 'Who?' Then Andrea: 'I don't know. Some woman.' Me again: 'A woman?'

'The only woman in Sydney who knows anything about this is Penny Draper,' Max said. 'And I'm absolutely positive she's straight.'

'She's *not* the only woman.' I told them about Claudia Vardon, how she'd turned up and that she lived in the Connaught.

'You say you didn't mention names, but,' Bob said.

'Yeah, but that time I was in her place, after we'd fucked, I went to sleep for a while. I had my notebook on me and I had Andrea Neville's name in it.'

'Shit,' Max said. 'That looks like it, but what's her angle?'

I was feeling too miserable and confused to think about it. Like anyone else, I'd been aroused and tempted by what was on display at Satisfaction, but at the back of my mind was the thought and prospect of Claudia. Now all that looked like turning into something very ugly. I forced myself to consider the ins and outs of it. If Claudia was Barry White's backer, was she also his killer? And had she made the attempt on Leo Grogan? All very unpleasant to contemplate but, as I faced it, the old curiosity began to take hold. And something more.

'I don't know what her angle could be,' I said quietly. 'But I'm going to find out.'

Bob saw my expression and tried for the light note. 'It's lucky you like beating up women,' he said.

'This one used me and made a fool of me. I don't like that one bit.'

Max coughed. 'When you're through being tough, we've got a couple of things to settle up here. We should see Sligo and we should try to get that note.'

My thoughts had gone straight back to Sydney, but I knew he was right. 'I wonder if he really is sick, or if he's got wind of things?'

'I called his office,' Bob said. 'They say he's got the flu. Had it a fair while. That tee time's a regular booking but apparently he hasn't played for weeks. Answering machine at his home number. The voice sounds a bit fluey you could say.'

I was in just the right mood for a sick, bent copper. 'Let's go and see him. You'd better stay clear of this, Bob. You have to live here.'

Bob nodded. 'Byron's more or less in my bailiwick. I know a few people down there. I could get some pressure applied to Andrea.'

'Good,' I said. 'Max and I'll go and see Sligo. Where's he live?'

'Pacific Towers, it's a high rise at the south end of the beach. Apartment 901.'

Bob patted his waist. 'The walk back'll do me good.'

The day had heated up and the tourists were out in force—pale legs and dark glasses, fat bellies and big behinds and some beautifully proportioned people of all races and both sexes. Max drove carefully through the light traffic and parked opposite the soaring tower block that would cast a shadow over the beach later in the day. He hadn't spoken since leaving the bar and I wondered about his mood.

'What's up, Max?'

'Do you feel we're getting any closer to finding out who killed Ramona Beckett? That's the object, remember? Especially from your point of view—that's where the money is.'

165

I was thinking along other lines and admitted it.

'I don't like losing the plot this much,' Max said.

'It probably all ties together in some way,' I said.

'And if it doesn't?'

'It wouldn't be the first time.'

'True,' Max said. 'Very true. I have a tendency to want to tie things up. It made me very unpopular in Adelaide with those people who liked things to stay untied.'

We crossed the road, skirted the palm trees in pots and went up the fake marble steps to the squawk boxes.

'I'll handle this,' Max said. 'I can usually hear these things for some reason.'

'I told Peggy Hawkins I'd try to keep her out of it.'

Max looked at me, shook his head and pressed the button for apartment 901.

'Yes.' A thick, husky voice.

'My name is Max Savage, Mr Sligo. I'm a senior investigating consultant with the New South Wales Police Force. I'd like to have a word with you.'

'What about?'

I mouthed the response but Max nodded impatiently. 'It's about information received from Sean Beckett, Wallace Cavendish, Andrea Craig and others about the Ramona Beckett case.'

The big plate glass doors slid open.

Colin Sligo was a big man, or he had been. He wore pyjamas, a paisley dressing gown and slippers, not an outfit to increase your presence, but there was clearly something wrong with him. He was stooped, he shuffled and it looked as if the gown had once fitted him better than it now did. He ushered us into a big living room with a dynamite view of the Pacific Ocean. He waved us into seats and sat with his back to it.

'Well?'

I launched into an edited version of what we were about and what we'd learned. His grey, flabby face scarcely changed as I spoke. He looked as if nothing I said could touch him and I worried that we were going to get nothing at all.

Sligo looked at Max. 'What've you got to say?'

'Nothing just now,' Max said. 'I'm waiting to hear from you.'

Sligo shrugged. 'You've got it all pretty well sorted out. Johnno knew I was coming up here and looking for a big score to take with me. I ran interference for him. Nothing much to it. Beckett paid well. Still does.'

'Not for much longer,' I said.

Sligo shrugged again. The slight movement seemed almost to exhaust him and he sat still after it for nearly a minute. 'I need a drink,' he said. 'Scotch, ice and water. Would you mind, Hardy? I'm pretty crook.'

I went across to a bar similar to the one at the brothel and made the drink. I looked at Max, who shook his head. I made a drink for myself. I was puzzled. I'd expected resistance, threats, bluster. In a way, this acquiescence was harder to deal with.

'Thanks,' Sligo said when I handed him the drink. 'What d'you want from me?'

Max leaned forward in his chair. 'The Craig woman says you put pressure on Beckett by saying you knew who'd done the kidnapping.'

'That's right. Johnno's idea. He was a smart cunt.'

'But you didn't know?' Max said.

Sligo shook his head and then obviously wished he hadn't. Just that movement caused him to sweat. He took a handkerchief from the pocket of the dressing gown and wiped his face. 'I didn't have a fucking clue. Neither did Johnno. Of course, we didn't even bother to look.'

I sipped my drink thinking this was very weird. I looked carefully at Sligo to see if there were any tricks he might pull. He certainly didn't have a weapon and there didn't seem to be any way he could summon assistance.

'Have you been keeping an eye on things in Sydney?' I asked. 'Got anyone down there working for you?'

'The only interest I've got in Sydney is in the horses and the football. Cavendish paid the money into an account regular as clockwork. There was nothing to watch. Tell you one thing, though.'

'What's that?' Max said.

'That Neville bitch, the one that used to be on the force, gave the ransom note to me.'

This was almost too much to handle. 'Why the fuck would she do that?' I said.

Sligo's face, flabby in some places, sunken in others, almost made it to a smile. 'You've gotta understand how much all these people hated each other—Johnno, Peg, me, Neville. We were all looking for the edge. Neville got the edge on Johnno but she reckoned she was safer giving me an edge on him, too. If Johnno ever sent anyone after her she'd tell them who had the note. It was all so fucking devious, no wonder it came unstuck. How *did* it come unstuck, anyway?'

'We don't know yet,' I said quickly. 'Where's the note?'

The almost smile had faded. Sligo sucked in a deep breath, apparently to give him the strength to get his glass to his mouth. 'I was part of the bloody game. It amused me that Johnno was sweating for years and paying through the nose for something that didn't exist. I burnt the fucking thing.'

'Describe it,' Max said.

'Oh, it was fair dinkum, I'd say. Not one of your TV bullshit things with cut-out newspaper and that crap. It was professionally typed and what I'd call stylish. I can't remember exactly what it said. Something about having abducted the girl and being prepared to let her live for two hundred thousand dollars.'

Max was taking notes. 'Who was it addressed to?'

Sligo scratched at his grey, flaky skin. 'The family, I think. I'm not sure.'

'What were the arrangements?'

'Jesus, it's a long time ago. None of your pick-up nonsense. The money was to be paid into a bank account and the girl'd be freed in a few days. You could do that back then—move large sums of money around, before the fucking government had its finger up everybody's arse.'

That much talking appeared to exhaust him and he sank back in his chair and sipped his drink.

'They had photocopiers back then,' I said. 'Are you sure you didn't make a few copies, for insurance?'

'I've told you. I burnt it and I fucking laughed while I did it.'

'You're not laughing now,' I said. 'In fact you're not much of anything. What's wrong with you, Mr Sligo?'

He drew in a deep breath and I could hear a rattle inside him that seemed to start in his lungs and come out through his throat. 'I've got cancer. Found out for sure two days ago, except I've really known it for weeks. I've got it everywhere. Probably got it in the dick, and I don't give a shit about you or Cavendish or Beckett or any fucking thing.'

19

Colin Sligo had never married and had no immediate family. He didn't care what revelations about him came out after he was dead which he said would be a matter of weeks if he didn't speed it up himself. He gave us the numbers of the bank account Cavendish had paid into on behalf of himself, Hawkins and the two women. He kept drinking steadily and was three parts drunk by the time we were ready to go.

'I still don't see what's in this for you, Hardy,' he said. 'It's ancient history.'

I couldn't see any harm in it so I told him about the reward.

He came as close as he could get to a laugh. 'Good luck. Good fucking luck.'

We drove back to Broadbeach and brought Bob up to scratch.

'So there's no need for you to go chasing hookers in Byron Bay,' Max said.

Bob nodded. 'Pity. I suppose you guys are keen to get back to the big smoke?'

Keen wasn't quite the word, but things needed doing. We booked a flight, thanked Bob and I told him to send a full account.

'You haven't got a client.'

'I'm going to collect the reward, remember? And if I don't I'm going to get something out of somebody.'

On the plane Max suddenly said. 'I never did get to meet my widow.'

'Pity,' I said. 'You'd have liked her. I did.'

At Mascot, Max and I agreed to talk later on the question of our next moves. Max went off to collect his thoughts and impressions and to contact Penny Draper. I got a cab to my office and checked the mail, fax and answering machines. There was nothing from Claudia. I phoned her number at the Connaught and got no reply, not even a machine. It was late in the day and, after the warmth of the Gold Coast, the air had a bite. That suited my mood. Carrying my overnight bag, I walked to the Connaught as quickly as I could, fuelled by anger.

I keyed her number in on the pad and got no answer. I beckoned to the desk attendant who pressed a button to unlock the door. That let me into an area that was still sealed off from the lifts. I could see what Claudia had meant about the security. I asked the attendant if he'd seen Ms Vardon recently.

'Ms Vardon?'

'Apartment 809.'

He consulted a booklet. 'That is not the name of the occupier.'

'I was in there a day ago. It's *her* apartment. OK, OK. *Who* is the occupier?'

'I'm afraid I can't tell you that, sir.'

I got out my PEA licence and showed it to him. He was very unimpressed. A fifty-dollar note didn't change his attitude and I went out onto the street seething with frustration. I stood on the spot where I'd bumped into her and could almost feel the force of her presence. I backed off to the street and stared up at the windows, remembering how she'd looked and felt and the hopes I'd had. I couldn't trust myself to talk to another human being, not even a cabbie. I slung the bag over my shoulder by its strap and walked home to Glebe.

No messages, no notes. I unpacked the bag, took a long shower and sat down with a large Scotch and my notebook, the one I assumed Claudia had investigated while I was asleep. I made my usual diagram with the broken and unbroken lines but my mind wasn't on the job. I wondered whether any of what she'd told me was true. Most wasn't. I put the pen and notebook down and worked on the Scotch. I realised that I'd dropped my guard way down. I hadn't even recorded the registration number of her car.

Images of her kept flashing into my mind. I've been told this happens when someone close to you dies. Well, that was fitting. The images were elusive, though, tangled up with vague memories of her laughter and sharp pictures of her face and movements. I scoured through the house in the hope that Claudia might have left something behind. I told myself I was doing this in the hope of finding some way to track her down, but I knew I was just looking for something to hold on to. I found nothing. I had another drink and, having skipped lunch after a busy morning and a bad afternoon, it hit me. I felt myself getting drunk and knew I should eat something but I had no appetite.

I was on my third drink when the phone rang. Just for a split second I thought it might be Claudia and I tried to marshall my thoughts.

'Cliff, this is Penny Draper.'

'Right.'

'Are you OK? Max wants to talk to you.'

'I'm not sure I want to talk to Max.'

A pause. I could imagine her mouthing my words. The thought irritated me and I slammed down the phone. *Fuck the disabled*, I thought. As soon as it formed, the thought seemed childish and I poised my hand over the phone waiting for the ring. I snatched it up.

'Penny? I'm sorry, I . . .'

'Another woman already? That's fast work, Cliff.'

It was Claudia's voice and I realised why Eve Crown hadn't been able to remember whether a man or a woman had made the call to Andrea. Claudia's voice was deep, almost masculine. Half-drunk, I was delighted by it and hated it at the same time.

'Aren't you going to say anything, Cliff?'

'Why are you doing this?'

'You mean ringing you now.'

I pressed the cold glass to my forehead. 'You know what I mean.'

'I suppose I do. I can't tell you just yet. I want you to know I admire you, though.'

'To hell with you. You lied to me from the first fucking minute.'

'That's right. I had my reasons.'

'Claudia, if that's your bloody name. One man's dead and another might as well be. Were there reasons for that.'

'I had nothing to do with that. I swear it.'

'I wish I could believe it. But how can I believe anything you say?'

'You want to though, don't you? We were good, Cliff. Weren't we good?'

'Stop it!'

'All right. Let's keep it businesslike if that's the way you want it. What's your next move?'

'You've got a nerve. Why would I tell you anything? I don't even know who you are.'

'That's right, you don't. And that's the way it has to stay for a while. But I can tell you this—everything you've done so far in this matter has been orchestrated by me. I sent Barry White to see you. And then I followed up myself. I enjoyed it, too. But you don't want to talk about that. My god, I nearly died when I bumped into you at the Connaught. And then you handed locating Barry's mystery contact right over to me.'

'That must have given you a laugh.'

'Not really. It was a lucky break, but if you're smart enough you create your own luck. You must know that.'

Despite all the rage inside me, I found myself enjoying talking to her. 'What's your interest in all this? Is it the reward?'

'No. I can't tell you but I will eventually. Right now, I need to know what happened up in Queensland. Did you see the Hawkins woman and Andrea Neville and Colin Sligo?'

'You take my bloody breath away. Yes, I saw them. But I'll be buggered if I'll tell you anything about it. Why should I?'

'You'll have to, sooner or later. Who was it, Cliff? Who suppressed the note? Was it Mrs Beckett, Sean, Estelle, Cavendish? Do you know?'

'No comment.'

'That's childish, after all I've done for you.'

She was steering me back in that direction again and I let myself be steered. I couldn't help it. 'Like what?'

'Didn't you wonder why the bashing you got was so ... gentle?'

'I wouldn't call it gentle. What d'you mean?'

'I wanted to test your resolve, Cliff. They went a bit too far, but I made it up to you, didn't I? Tell me you haven't thought about it since. Tell me you haven't thought about having your cock in my mouth. Tell me you're not thinking about it right now?'

'I'm thinking you're a crazy, manipulative, lying bitch ...'

'With a lovely tight cunt.'

I was sober now, or close to it, and able to think. I tried to turn this weird contact to my advantage but couldn't see how. I said nothing.

'Stony silence. OK. Do whatever you like. You won't get far. I'll call again this time tomorrow and maybe you'll be more reasonable.'

'Claudia, don't . . .'

She hung up and I slammed the phone down again. It rang straight off and I let it ring for a long time. When I picked up Penny Draper sounded very peeved.

'I thought you must've left the phone off the hook. You were very rude, before, Cliff.'

'I'm sorry,' I said. 'I really can't talk to Max just now. I have to get some sleep and straighten things out in my head. I'll ring at nine tomorrow. OK?'

I hung on while she communicated this to Max. I expected her to speak again but it was Max himself on the line.

'Cliff, I understand you've got some problems. OK. Just wanted to tell you that Cavendish has gone to Melbourne for a day. They work late in that game and his secretary told me. He's our best way into this thing as I see it. Not much we can do till he gets back. We'll talk tomorrow. Come in here about ten. Goodnight.'

He hung up and I stood there with my hand cramping around the phone.

I had to bend down to shake Penny Draper's hand and I have no doubt she would have been able to flip me over the back of the wheelchair if she'd wanted to. She was a solidly built, dark-haired woman in her thirties. Her face was pleasant and just missed being plain. She wore eye make-up and lipstick and knew how to apply them for best effect. She wore a white blouse, dark trousers and flat-heeled shoes. At a guess, she did weight training—her shoulders were developed and her grip was strong. Short nails, no rings.

'I'm glad to meet you, Cliff,' she said. 'Max thinks a lot of you.'

'Hello, Penny. Sorry I was so shitty last night. I'd been put off-balance.'

'Fatal in any game,' she said. 'Don't worry about it. Max isn't in yet, surprisingly, or maybe not. Can I get you a cup of coffee?'

We were deep in the bowels of the Darling-hurst police complex in a small office that had two smaller rooms attached to it. The service, evidently, did not give great weight to its consultant investigative unit. The outfit had two computers and lots of paper. In the important divisions these days, it's the other way around. I suppressed the normal impulse to refuse when a cripple offers to do anything for you.

'Thanks, Penny. Some coffee'd be good. White, no sugar.'

She wheeled swiftly across to a table where the urn and fixings were set out and did the business briskly. I looked around the room, noting the orderliness and efficiency. Schedules and lists were pinned to noticeboards; a big whiteboard was covered in diagrams and notes; a scale model of a building was showing on one of the computer screens while options like 'dimensions', 'colour', 'entrance', 'exit', flashed enticingly. The coffee was good. I leaned against a desk while Penny answered a phone.

When she'd finished I said, 'You suggested that maybe it's not surprising that Max isn't here. What did you mean by that?'

She picked up a pencil and tapped on the desk with it for a minute. Then she put it back. 'Have you ever been disabled, Cliff? Put out of action for a while?'

I nodded. 'I had an eye injury. I was effectively blind for a bit.'

'Right. Did you notice an increased sensitivity to sound and smell and all that, the way the books say?'

'I did, yes. It went away when I could see again.'

'Did you have a partner at the time?'

Helen Broadway, I thought. *Yes, by god I did.* I nodded.

'Touch became important, right? And smell and taste?'

'That's right.' I had no idea where this was heading, but it made me feel vaguely uncomfortable. I sipped the coffee and wished Max would come.

'Well, it's like that with me since . . . this happened. I can read people's body language, pick up things from the way they move, the tone of voice, the balance of positive and negative in what they do. D'you understand?'

'What's this about, Penny.'

179

'If you asked Max why he's late he'd say he was giving us a few minutes to get to know each other. But that's only partly true. What he's *really* doing is using you as a way of finding out what I think of him. Is that too devious for you?'

'A bit. Yes.'

'I'm in love with him. I have been since the first day. He's smart and funny and not vain. He's stubborn about his deafness and the most understanding person I've met about my condition. I'm crazy about him. I want him very badly.'

'Penny, I . . .'

'I can have sex, you know. Everything's all right down there. Masturbate. It's fine. It'd take a little ingenuity but I reckon Max is an ingenious enough man. You're embarrassed. I understand. But just hear me out. Pretty soon, Max will ask you what you think of me and then he'll sidle round to asking what I think of him. He will, believe me.'

'OK. I believe you. What d'you want me to do?'

'Tell him.'

'It's my turn to read minds. He'll say he's nearly twice your age.'

'So he's got twenty years and I've got forty. Say we had twenty together. I'd settle for that.'

Max strode into the room and dropped his briefcase with a thud. 'Hello, you two. How're you getting along?'

20

Coffee all round. Penny went to work at the computer. Max and I huddled in a corner. I told him about the phone call from Claudia Vardon.

'She's the key to the whole thing, Max.'

'Hold on, hold on. We could be getting our wires crossed here. The whole thing, for me, is the suppression of evidence, the corruption of police officers, the cover-up of a major crime. Plus . . .'

'The murder of Ramona Beckett.'

'Exactly. We've got a handle on the first parts of it, with or without your mystery lady.'

'Not much of a one as things stand. A tape of some women talking dirty.'

'Don't mumble. You're giving yourself away. What was that you said?'

'All we've got is a tape of some women talking in a brothel.'

'Wrong. I taped Sligo. I meant to tell you that. You heard what he said. It was virtually a death-bed testimony. That's pretty powerful stuff. You're getting sidetracked by this woman. Women can do that better than men.'

I couldn't help trying to steer him in the direction Penny had pointed. 'Is that right, Max? You'd know, would you?'

He didn't bite. 'Save the irony. Cavendish is the target.'

Against every logical instinct I wanted to play it the way Claudia outlined. '*She*, this Claudia Vardon woman, knows more about all this than we know.'

'Jesus, you're obsessed. OK, so what do you want to do?'

'How's this? You and Penny find out everything you can about Sean Beckett. When we tackle him we're going to need some ammunition unless he just goes to pieces. That's a day's work. Claudia rings tonight. If nothing comes of that we go up against the lot of them with whatever we've got.'

'What will you be doing?'

'I'll do the same on Cavendish. I've got a few mates in the legal game. I'll look in on Leo Grogan if that's possible.'

'It feels like marking time.'

'Make some copies of the tapes. Check on the bank accounts. Check on whether anything's turned up on the Barry White hit. Since we don't think there's anyone here keeping an eye on us, you can do that. Come on, Max, you're a copper. You know the drill. Background, mate, background.'

Max looked over to where Penny was working and from the expression on his face I got the feeling that she'd read him exactly right. His lean face softened and there was something wistful in the tilt of his head. Or was I imagining it? She sat very straight in the wheelchair. Her thick dark hair was brushed back, revealing small, delicate ears and a shapely neck. Maybe Max was a neck man.

He nodded. 'All right.'

I cupped my ear. 'Speak up!'

Max laughed. 'You bastard.'

Penny looked across and smiled. I gave her a thumbs up and left them to it.

Leo Grogan had been transferred to a private hospital in Marrickville. Against the odds, and to the surprise of the medicos, he'd survived the crisis and was on the way to at least a partial recovery. There was some doubt as to whether he'd gain the full use of his left side but, as Leo drank with his right arm, I doubted that this would worry him too much. I got this information from an obliging nurse at the hospital where I represented myself as a relative.

'Poor Mr Grogan hasn't had any visitors,' the nurse said. 'He'll be glad to see you.'

'I'm sure he will.' I meant it. I had a half bottle of Johnny Walker red in my pocket. I don't like hospitals. People die in them and have bits removed, so I went as quickly as I could through to the ward which Leo shared with two other men. He was sitting up watching television. His head was bandaged and there were a couple of tubes running into his left upper arm.

'Uncle Leo, my favourite uncle,' I said. 'How're you getting along?'

'What the fuck're you doing here, Hardy?'

'Is that any way to greet your one and only visitor?' I pulled the curtain half around, shielding us off from the other two patients, both of whom had their televisions going. Leo looked alarmed until I produced the bottle. He nodded vigorously and pointed to the tray carrying a water carafe and two glasses. I switched off the TV, poured two solid shots, added water and put the whisky in the top drawer of his bedside table under a pair of pyjamas.

Leo put half of his drink down in a gulp. 'You're a lifesaver. Now what the fuck do you want?'

'Same old Leo. Oh, not much. Just keeping you up to date on the investigation that might still pay off big for us.'

'It's *us* now is it? That's all bullshit, Hardy.'

'Maybe. Did you know Barry White was dead?'

Leo finished his drink and reached for the drawer. I held it shut. He rolled his eyes. 'I might've known. Yeah, I heard about Barry. I guess Rinso finally got him, eh?'

'Rinso?'

'Give us another drink and I'll tell you about it. Truth is I was never too happy about spending time with Barry like I'd been doing lately in case Rinso turned up.'

I was all at sea and another violation of hospital rules seemed the only way to enlightenment. I made Grogan another drink and sipped my own while he told me about the long-running feud between Freddy 'Rinso' Persil and Barry White. Apparently White had got Persil's daughter hooked on heroin, had supplied her and used her and sold her the junk that had killed her. Persil was in gaol at the time, but he'd sworn to kill White. According to Grogan, he was released three days before White was shot. I tried to think back to White's panicked phone call. I'd assumed then that what was alarming him had to do with the Beckett case, but that was just an assumption.

'What's the matter, Hardy,' Grogan mocked. 'Some sweet theory gone out the fucking window?'

'Maybe. What about you, Leo. Who gave you the heave-ho?'

He laughed. 'Nobody. I was pissed and I fell down the fucking steps. Lucky I've got this good hospital insurance. Part of my package. They reckon I might be partly paralysed but that's bullshit. Between you and me, I'm faking it a bit so's they'll keep on their toes.'

His second drink was gone and he was looking at the drawer again. I was having mixed feelings. If all this was true, then Claudia was off the hook as an actual and would-be killer. But could Grogan be trusted? Then something he'd said came back to me.

'Leo, you said you'd been spending time with Barry White lately. I only heard about two meetings—sounds like there was a few more.'

'You're a prize prick, Hardy, but you're not

dumb. Yeah, there was another meeting. Give me another drink and I'll tell you about it. Make it quick, they'll be coming around to feed us some fucking slop soon.'

I gave Leo a weaker drink and showed him what was left in the bottle before putting it back in the drawer. He nodded and took a more judicious sip.

'This woman came to see me. What she didn't know about the fucking Beckett case wasn't worth knowing. She knew I'd been on the team and she asked me if I knew anything, anything at all, that was off about the investigation. Well, I hadn't thought about it for years, but I remembered that scene between Johnno and Peg, just like I told it to you.'

'For the second time,' I said.

Leo swigged his drink. He was feeling pleased with himself now. 'For the fucking third time. We get together again and this time she's got Barry White along. I go through it again. Then she sets up the meeting with you and Barry and I have to act it out the way Barry told you it happened.'

'I never knew coppers were such good actors.'

'Are you kidding? You have to be, the fucking bullshit you have to say in court and write down and tell the brass, not to mention the crims, gets you that way. Anyway, that's it. I asked for a monkey and I got it. She and Barry set you up to do whatever you fucking did. And you still haven't told me what that was.'

186

'You say she knew everything about the case. What do you mean?'

'I mean every fucking thing. All about the girl who went missing, the family, the lot. It seemed to me she wasn't even surprised when I told her about the note and that. It was as if she already knew about it.'

'So, do you think she was a secretary to the old man, or the mother, or worked for the lawyer, or something like that?'

'Be buggered,' Leo said. 'I reckon she was one of the kidnappers, or knew them, and she'd come up with a way to have a go at the reward money.'

'Took her a long time.'

Leo shrugged. 'Playing safe. Maybe something changed in the set-up. Maybe she'd finally decided it was time to dob someone in.'

'Yeah, maybe.'

'They're late with the fucking lunch.'

'I thought you said it was slop.'

'It is, but it breaks up the day.' He raised his almost empty glass. 'It'll go down a bit better with this inside me.'

'Watch out they don't smell your breath.' I took a deep breath myself and asked the question I'd been holding back. 'What did she look like, Leo, this woman.'

'Fucking good-looker, Hardy. Too good for you.'

'Be specific.'

Leo shrugged and his flabby jowls bounced.

'Tallish, great figure, good tits and arse, everything. She wore big dark glasses and that sort of makes it hard to describe her face.'

'Hair?'

'Dark. Funny thing was, I kept feeling that I'd met her before.'

21

Marrickville Park is my kind of place—a big, open space, roughly mown with a football oval, plenty of trees, not too many flowers and some grass tennis courts tucked away in one corner. The croquet lawn in the opposite corner is a bit of an anomaly, but live and let live. You don't see grass tennis courts much any more. They remind me of the great days of Australian tennis—Hoad and Rosewall, Laver and Emerson, Newcombe and Roche. They weren't such great days in other ways—Bob Menzies, six o'clock closing, Vietnam—but I yearn for them sometimes when I hear about crack and child pornography and the hole in the ozone layer.

I parked in Frazer Street and wandered through the park to the courts, kicking at pine cones. I was having trouble being objective about this twisting, turning mess of a case I had on my hands. I'd started out greedy for a hundred thousand dollars, had entertained thoughts of a whole lot more money and now was mostly hoping that Claudia Vardon, or whatever her name was, wasn't too deep in the criminal soup. Who was I to be judgmental? I'd recently killed a man, falsified evidence and served a gaol term. As a private investigator I was more or less on probation. My personal needs were greater than my professional standards and I knew it. Had always known it.

Two good players were on the courts—a baseliner and net-rusher. The baseliner had a double-fisted backhand like Agassi and the serve–volleyer had obviously modelled his game on Edberg's. It had always seemed to me that a serve–volley player should beat a baseliner because that game requires a high passage over the net—easy meat for the volleyer. It hadn't proved true over the years, but here on a suburban court, with a couple of fit A-graders at work, it was. The surface made the difference. The grass took the Edberg-style underspin and flat shots and kept the ball low. The Agassi clone couldn't get topspin on either side and had to hit up. Stefan was there at the net and Andre was dead. I felt like applauding. But it would be like applauding the dinosaurs. I'd read that less than 5 per cent of professional tennis is played on grass these days.

I wasn't convinced that Claudia was one of the kidnappers, or an associate of one. It didn't seem to fit. Against that, Peggy Hawkins was certainly just such a player in the game. Why not someone similar from the opposing side that turned out to be unopposed? It was all confused by my feelings for her which were mixed to say the very least. The strong sexual attraction had to be balanced against the ruthless way she'd used and manipulated me. My ribs were still sore and I still had sutures in my torn ear and I felt humiliated about being delivered home like a gift-wrapped package. I had a strong wish to meet up with those three blokes again with the odds better balanced.

As I watched the balls go over the net and hit the fences with the force good players can generate, I realised that the best way to resolve all my dilemmas was to act like the volleyer—take the high ground and the initiative. I had to try to find Claudia Vardon before she phoned me and started calling the shots all over again. It *had* to be Claudia who'd met with Leo Grogan and set the ball rolling. The dark hair was no problem.

It seemed reasonable to begin in Glebe. She appeared to be able to keep track of my movements there. She'd certainly known when I'd got back the other night. Most likely she'd just driven past, but if her intention was to keep really close tabs on me there was a chance she was staying somewhere nearby. There are no flash hotels in Glebe, just good, serviceable motels like the Rooftop and the Haven Inn on Glebe Point Road and the University Motor Inn across the way from what it gets its name from. I'm quite well known in all three of them, especially the Rooftop where I've occasionally put witnesses and other parties who needed putting. It has a swimming pool where you'd imagine—a big plus in summer and, besides, anxious people like to be able to go up on a roof and look down on the world that's giving them a hard time.

I did a quick check on the motels, giving them my description of Claudia and the car. Three blanks. I extended the search to Chippendale and Camperdown but came up with the same result. I couldn't see Claudia staying in a backpacker hostel. The Blackwattle Bay end of Glebe is full of blocks of flats and flats become available for short-term leases and sub-lets. Claudia's operation had obviously been well-planned, so securing a second base in advance wasn't out of the question. More in hope than expectation, I toured the streets and looked in on the car parks. I knew a few of the residents and could ask them later, but the more I carried out this exercise, the more I realised I was kidding myself. She was too smart to be found by the equivalent of turning over rocks.

I went home to find a message from Max on the answering machine. The house seemed emptier and more desolate in the day than at night. The empty rooms and the bachelor routines I mostly enjoyed felt like signs of failure and put me in a bad mood. I phoned and got ready to go into the usual routine with Penny.

'Penny, this is Cliff. Max wants to talk to me.'

'And *I* want to talk to you. Did he say anything.'

'About what?'

'About me! Who d'you think?'

I hadn't given it any thought since my attempt to read Max's body language. That was too slim a foundation to make a comment on, and after my wasted effort I wasn't feeling obliging. 'No, nothing.'

'He will. I'll put him on.'

I wished I could feel as optimistic as Penny and I was feeling more sour by the minute when Max came on the line.

'I've been onto that Redfern D—Fowler. He says . . .'

'A guy named Freddy Persil shot Barry. I got all that from Grogan.'

A pause, then Penny's voice, choked with anger. 'Don't do that, Cliff! You know he can't hear you. Why're you screwing him up like that?'

'I'm sorry, Penny. I haven't had a good morning. Look, I've found out a few useful things. I'll put them in a fax.'

'Why won't you talk?' she said angrily. 'Wait on, Max! I'm trying to . . .'

Everyone was getting shirty. 'To tell you the truth, I find this method of communication bloody difficult. Let's be up to date about this. Tell Max to fax me what he wants to tell me and I'll do the same.'

She hung up in my ear.

I felt shitty about it, but then, I felt shitty generally. I made a drink and wrote out a fax giving Max the gist of what I'd learned from Leo Grogan. I tried to be objective, listing the only two possible connections Claudia could have to the Becketts— that she was a former confidential employee of Cavendish or associated with the kidnappers. I favoured the first option and said so. I stressed that, in my opinion, working through her was the best way to progress. I didn't say that I'd spent hours wandering around Glebe looking for her.

I sent the fax and went up the street for some more wine and whisky and food which, for me, generally means fruit, bread, eggs and anything else my eye lights on. My mood improved on the walk and I exchanged greetings with a few of the shopkeepers and spent more money than I'd intended. I was contemplating replying to Max's communication with an apology when I approached the house and saw something fluttering on my windscreen. *Another carpet cleaner*, I thought. I put the carry bags down on the hood and plucked the paper from under the wipers. I unfolded the sheet of yellow legal foolscap. The message, in bold, flowing felt tip, read: 'Nice try, Cliff. Call you tonight at 9. C.'

It could have gone either way. I could have been furious at her arrogance and my incompetence or been amused at the cheekiness of it, the gall. The second way won, but my reaction was perverse. I realised that I was glad to have had her watching me. As far as I recalled I hadn't picked my nose or spat on the pavement. I looked up and down the street, half expecting her to be there, laughing at me. She wasn't, of course, but she could have been in any of the cars that had been on the road. Dark hair, dark glasses, the Laser was probably hired, so a different car. Why not?

A taxi turned into the street, one of those taxis with a high roof. It pulled in behind my car and Max got out. He helped the driver run Penny's wheelchair down the ramp and onto the pavement. Max gave the cabbie a card and as he was running it through, the wheelchair came purring towards me.

'Hello, Penny.'

'Cliff. We decided not to let this bullshit go any further.'

'That's good. I was mentally composing an apology fax.'

Penny gestured at the paper in my hand. 'What's that you've got there?'

'I'll explain inside over a drink.' The taxi drove away and Max came up to stand proprietorially behind the wheelchair. 'Gidday, Max. I've just invited Penny in for a drink. You can come too if you like.'

'Where she goes, I go.'

I looked at Penny. 'Ah,' I said.

Max frowned. 'What's the mean?'

'Private joke,' I said. 'I thought you were only interested in widows.'

'Max?' Penny said.

I opened the gate. 'Another private joke. I win. After youse.'

Terrace houses are not wheelchair-friendly, but we had no trouble getting Penny inside and installed in the living room with a glass of wine in her hand. Something had clearly happened between them, but for the moment Max, who accepted a small Scotch, was all business.

'We're got a lot of dope on Sean Beckett,' he said. 'Apparently, he's a nutter.'

'Max,' Penny said. 'That's inaccurate.'

'All right. A neurotic; unstable, disturbed, whatever you want to call it.'

I drank some Scotch and wondered when Claudia would call and how to handle it. I tried to concentrate on what Max was saying but it was hard. 'I've been called unstable and disturbed myself. Don't know about neurotic. What're the signs in his case?'

'His marriage broke up—guess when? Immediately after the Beckett thing.'

'Marriages break up,' I said. 'Mine for one.'

'Sorry, I didn't know that. How long ago?'

'I forget. Long time. OK. What else?'

'He's been in therapy ever since. He's a raving hypochondriac, spends a fortune on doctors and health cures. He's obese, really huge. I've got a picture of him, look.'

Max took an envelope from his pocket and showed me a grainy photo of a very fat man. Two chins rested on his tie knot.

'Could be genetic,' I said. 'We don't know anything about his mum.'

'Yes, we do. She was an accountant, helped old man Beckett get his start. She died not long after the divorce. Here she is, and the daughter.'

Penny was looking around the room, maybe noting the cobwebs and frayed carpet, maybe wondering if the bookshelves could take much more of a load before collapsing. I'd wondered that myself.

'You've been busy,' I said.

Max sipped his Scotch. 'Penny has.'

More photos. A pleasant-faced woman, kept from being attractive by close-set eyes that gave her an owlish look. Estelle Beckett favoured her father, who was a handsome man. The picture was a studio portrait and probably flattering. She had good bone structure and even features and knew how to use cosmetics and how to pose to make the best of them. She was good-looking but not a patch on Ramona which, as she projected vanity and self-absorption, must have been a problem for her. No suggestion of a weight problem, though.

'OK,' I said. 'Sean's a very troubled individual.'

Penny glanced across at me. 'That's almost civilised.'

Max took the photos back and tucked them away. 'He's on the board of this and that, as the mother told you, but he's worse than useless. He was managing director of a couple of things for a while but people had to step in to prevent them from going bottom up. He rakes in more money than you and I can imagine, but for all that he's a . . . what was it, Pen?'

'A cipher,' Penny said.

22

I made scrambled eggs on toast and we ate, drank wine and waited for Claudia's call. I set the recording device to start taping the second she spoke and I brought the upstairs phone down and plugged it in at the kitchen so Penny and I could both listen. The phone rang at nine o'clock precisely.

'Cliff, who're those people you've got with you? And don't lie to me.'

'That's a bad start, Claudia. Where are you?'

'Not far away but you'd never find me. Oh, maybe you would if you had a week or so, but this is all going to be over well before that.'

'What is?'

'Come on, I answered your question and gave you some information. Give a little. If they're technicians to trace the call I'm disappointed in you. That's unimaginative.'

I was standing in the doorway to the living room with the kitchen phone at full stretch. I could see Penny on the other phone mouthing the dialogue to Max. He was nodding. They were doing more than communicating, they were communing. Both disabled, but I envied them.

'You know how to appeal to my vanity,' I said. 'They're not technicians. The man is Max Savage, he's a consultant to the police, investigating old cases. The woman is his assistant. They're friends of mine.'

'That's interesting. I look forward to meeting them. Having a few drinks are you, something to nibble?'

'Claudia, what the hell . . . ?'

'Humour me. I've been dieting for weeks. Oh, forget it. Look, Cliff, I want you to set up a meeting between Mrs Beckett, Wallace Cavendish and you and me. You can bring your friends along if you like.'

'That might not be easy. Cavendish . . .'

'Will be waiting for your call. He'll agree, believe me.'

'How many people can you manipulate all at once, Claudia?'

'Plenty, if I have to. Arrange with Cavendish to meet tomorrow night out at that godawful place in Wollstonecraft. Nine o'clock, say.'

'Are you sure you don't want Sean Beckett there, and Estelle. How about I fly Peggy Hawkins down from the Gold Coast?'

'Very funny.'

I was tired of being the wall against which the ball was being bounced. 'The working theory at this end, Claudia, is that you're associated in some way with the people who kidnapped and killed Ramona Beckett. Anything to contribute?'

'No, please just do as I say.'

'It's please, now, is it? Why don't you come along to my place and meet Max and Penny? We don't really like getting run around the block like this. Tell you what, you come here and we'll tell you what you want to know—who suppressed the kidnapping note.'

'I'm sorry, Cliff. It has to be this way. You can tell me that tomorrow night.'

'Terrific. By the way, will I get the reward, too? The fucking pot of gold.'

She hung up on me, the second woman to do it in one day. *Great going, Cliff.*

Penny replaced the receiver and turned off the tape-recorder. I came back into the room with the whisky and wine and refreshed my drink and Max's. Penny accepted some more wine.

'Your telephone manner stinks,' she said, addressing me but facing Max.

'She got under my skin. I'm sick of being manipulated and all this mystery woman shit.'

'Male ego challenged.'

'If you like.'

Max said, 'I think I got most of it from Pen, but was there anything said that gives us a better idea of what's going on?'

Penny and I shook our heads. 'Not even worth playing the tape,' I said.

Penny sipped her wine. 'I'd say she's an Australian who's lived in the States for a while. What was that about dieting? Is she fat, Cliff?'

'No.'

'Thin?'

'No.'

'What?'

'In between.'

'Jesus, men!'

'Look, she's a beautiful woman, but she's forty or thereabouts. She's not a girl or one of those anorexic models. She's got a woman's figure. I can't see any reason why she'd want to diet. Anyway, she's lying. She ate her share the night we had a meal together.'

'I can't see any reason why she'd want to do anything she's done,' Max said. 'I'm completely in the dark. Did you do any digging on Cavendish? Turn up former employees and so on?'

It was one of the things I'd been supposed to do and I hadn't even thought about it. I shook my head.

Max looked peeved. 'We need to get some leverage on this woman. As it is, she's making all the running.'

'But she wants to know what we know,' Penny said. 'About the suppression of the note. That seems to be the one thing she doesn't have. You don't seem to be her favourite person, Cliff.'

I knew what Penny was up to with that statement. She was going to get a read from my expression and body language. I tried to keep both as neutral as I could. 'I'm nobody's favourite person right now, including my own.'

'On that bright note I think we might take our leave, Pen,' Max said. 'Thanks for the drinks and tucker, Cliff.'

I called for a wheelchair-equipped taxi and

we had a bit of a wait. The conversation was desultory but friendly. We'd healed the breach right enough and Max and Penny had done a whole lot more in that direction. We loaded the wheelchair into the taxi and Max and I shook hands.

'I'll ring you tomorrow afternoon,' I said. 'I might have something on Cavendish by then. And we can talk about what to do tomorrow night. That's if she's right—if Cavendish agrees to a meeting and can arrange it with Mrs Beckett.'

Max nodded. 'She seemed very sure it'd play like that. I wonder why she's so confident?'

I shrugged. 'I've never seen her any other way, except maybe angry. She's not a person with doubts.'

Max glanced in to where Penny was sitting patiently. 'A person without doubts has no imagination. Goodnight, Cliff.'

The taxi drove off and I stood in the street for a while speculating about where Claudia might be. There were no high-rises overlooking my spot, nowhere for her to take up a position with binoculars. Then it hit me—the house for sale on the other side of the street, the one she'd ostensibly been interested in buying. I went inside, got a torch and my lock-picks and walked down towards the house. It was a double-fronted timber job that had been on the market for quite some time. Unusually for the area, it had a deep front garden and a driveway of sorts. To judge by the state of the weeds, the double gates to the drive, which was fringed by overgrown shrubs, had been opened recently and a car had been parked inside.

The lock on the front door was an old Yale, easy to pick. I had it open inside a minute and stepped into the hallway. The house had a cloying, moist, musty smell indicating rising damp. If the vendors had put a high price on it, buyers would have been deterred by the smell. I went into the first room on the left. The street rose sharply beyond my place. From the front window of this house, which was set up on high foundations, the view back to my gate and the side of my house was clear. The room was devoid of furniture, but an old bentwood chair had been placed by the window. Two of the panes had been cleaned. Two styrofoam coffee cups sat on the dusty boards beside the chair. My respect for Claudia Vardon went up a few more notches.

I went back, half hoping that she'd be there, standing in the doorway or sitting in a chair in the living room. She wasn't, of course. I washed the glasses, plates and frying pan and made some coffee. I sat and played the tape through but learned nothing new from it. *Great voice*, I found myself thinking uselessly.

It wasn't late and I wasn't tired. I went for a walk about the block and strolled down to the water below the big apartment complex at the end of the street. The grass had recently been cut and the fresh-mown smell was strong and pleasant as I sucked in deep breaths and did a mental review of the whole Ramona Beckett matter. The lights of the city skyline shone in the still water like a distorted duplicate of the real thing. The more I thought about the case the more it seemed that we hadn't been grappling with reality but with some kind of shadow or mirage. Suddenly, I *was* tired, mentally and physically, and I tossed a couple of stones into the water to break up the image and went home.

The light on the answering machine was blinking. I hit the play button, knowing for certain whose voice it would be.

'Smart work, Cliff,' she said. 'I knew you were the right man for the job. See you tomorrow.'

23

Mrs Horsfield's voice was still the same soothing instrument when she answered the phone at ten o'clock the following day. 'Good morning, Mr Hardy,' she intoned. 'I was told to expect a call from you.'

That was encouraging so I thought I'd take a punt. 'Would you mind telling me how long you've worked for Mr Cavendish, Mrs Horsfield?'

'Not at all. More than twenty years.'

'In that time I suppose there would have been a good many associates, para-legals, secretaries and so on in the office.'

'Certainly.'

'Do you recall a woman named Claudia? A qualified solicitor?'

'No.'

'You're sure?'

'I'm quite sure. Mr Cavendish has never employed females in responsible positions other than myself.'

Couldn't make it any more plain than that. I thanked her and waited to be put through to Wally the sexist. When he came on the line he sounded tired and worn, half the man he used to be.

'Hardy,' he said, as if even that was an effort.

'You don't sound well, Mr Cavendish. But then I expect you're in better condition than Colin Sligo.'

No response.

'You do know Sligo, don't you?'

'You know perfectly well I do.'

'He's dying of cancer. He saw no reason not to tell me everything I wanted to know.'

'Ah, I see. Yes, that makes some kind of sense.'

'Have you been in touch with Sean Beckett recently?'

'I have no intention of submitting to any interrogation by you. Certainly not at this time.'

That appeared to leave the door wide open so I took the step. 'I want to arrange a meeting . . .'

His sigh came down the line like a gust of dry wind. 'For tonight at nine o'clock at Wollstonecraft with Mrs Beckett and other parties whose identities I haven't been given. I've had my instructions. It's all arranged.'

'Instructions? Who from?'

'From whom? From Mrs Beckett, naturally.' He hung up.

Trouble at the ranch, I thought. *Mrs Beckett now, not Gabriella*. I wandered around the house in track pants, T-shirt and sneakers for a few minutes mulling this over. It had rained during the night and I went out onto the balcony off my bedroom to see if some fresh-washed air would help the thinking process. My thinking changed course abruptly when I saw the red 4WD with the silver mudflaps turn into the lane that runs off my street. I knew from my years of walking around the area that you could get a clear view of the back and front of my house from a point along that lane. I also knew where I'd seen that vehicle, or one like it, before—in Wollstonecraft, being exited by a man with an aluminium baseball bat in his hand.

I took my .38 Smith & Wesson from its holster in the hall cupboard, checked it over and wrapped it in a plastic shopping bag so that I could carry it in my hand, ready to fire, but not alarm the neighbours. I went out the back door, hunched down behind my neighbour's over-grown rubber tree and kicked out three palings in the fence. I went through the gap and across his yard. I couldn't be seen from the high point of the lane there, and the neighbour's back gate was never locked. I went through it and was now in a position to work through the streets and come out above where the Pajero would be parked if watching my place was his game.

It was there, bullbars, silver mudflaps and all. The driver was standing in front of the vehicle, shading his eyes and looking down towards my house. I had no doubt it was the same guy—same height, same compact build. I hugged the fence, stayed in the shadows and came up behind him, dead quiet in sneakers on the bitumen. When I got closer I could see that his jaw was in constant movement as he chewed. I was beside the Pajero now and sneaked a glance inside. Cigarettes, a lighter and a mobile phone on the seat, no baseball bat. I was almost disappointed. I reached in, took the lighter and lobbed it over his head.

He froze just long enough as it landed and took just long enough turning for me to get around the hood of the car and slam the barrel of the .38 onto the bridge of his nose. He screamed. The bone gave and the front sight dug into his cheek just below his eye. Blood flowed from the nose and the cheek and he threw his hands up to his face. The chewing gum flew from his mouth. I backed off a step, hoping there'd be some fight in him. After all, he wasn't to know that what I'd hit him with was a gun. He recovered quickly and came at me, but his eyes were full of tears and he had no judgment of distance. I let him get within punching reach before I stepped aside and hit him again, this time catching him along the side of the jaw. The skin split along the bone. I kicked his left knee inwards and he went down, banging his battered head against the side of the car.

I took the plastic from the gun, crouched down next to him and put the barrel in the hollow just below his prominent Adam's apple. His face was a mask of blood. He'd bitten his tongue and blood was seeping from his mouth along with the scent of Juicy Fruit.

'Where is she?' I said.

'You've taken my fucking eye out.'

'No, it's all right. A couple of stitches and you'll be good as new. Same as me with my ear. Where is she?'

'Who?'

'Don't be brave, mate. Don't be brave.'

'You wouldn't shoot me.'

'Right. I wouldn't, seeing as how I've got you down like this. I'm not licensed to carry the gun at the moment and I wouldn't want to get in that sort of trouble. But I'd be happy to break your arm.'

'Bullshit.'

It's easier to do than you'd think, especially if you're quick. I was crouched and balanced, he was sprawled and had no leverage. I dropped the gun so that it landed heavily in his crotch. He yelped. I picked up his limp left arm and snapped it across my knee midway between the wrist and elbow. He opened his mouth to yell and I filled it with the blood-streaked plastic carry bag. I held it there until he was gasping for breath.

'Now I'll do the other one if you like, which'd be worse because it's your right. But I don't want to, so where is she?'

I retrieved the gun and took the bag away. He gulped in air and babbled. 'I don't know. Swear I don't know. Swear I don't know. I phone her. Just phone. I just phone . . .'

'OK. On the mobile?'

He nodded and blood ran freely from his nose. He sniffed it up and started to gag. I found a couple of crumped tissues in my pocket and gave them to him. 'Stay here,' I said.

I got the mobile and the cigarettes from the car, picked up the lighter and crouched down again. 'What's your name?'

'Bruce, Bruce . . .'

'Bruce'll do. Have you called her recently, Bruce?'

'Just now.'

'Good.' I put the cigarettes and lighter down within reach of his good arm and hit the redial button on the phone. It rang briefly and she answered.

'Yes?' she said.

'This is Cliff, Claudia. I've just had a meeting with Bruce and he's not feeling too well. If you were planning to bring him along tonight I think you'd better get someone else.'

'I wasn't. Not necessary.'

'Well, you know where he is. I'd suggest you phone for an ambulance. I don't think he's up to driving just now.'

I hung up. It was good to do it myself for a change.

There was blood on my clothes and shoes. I put the gun back in the cupboard, stripped off and showered. The bruises on my ribs were fading and the sutures in my ear were on the way to dissolving. I could wash my hair without having to be too gentle about the side of my head. I'd hurt men worse than I'd hurt Bruce in my time and been hurt worse myself. I didn't feel anything in particular about it. He'd go on doing what he did and I'd do the same, there was nothing more to it.

I rang Max's office. He was out but Penny was in. I told her about the conversations with Cavendish and Mrs Horsfield.

'So we're set?' Penny said.

'Looks like it.'

'It's all a bit weird, isn't it? Perhaps we should have some back-up.'

I told her about the meeting with Bruce, omitting some of the details, and Claudia's assurance that *she* wouldn't have any support troops.

'You believe her?'

'Yes.'

'Why?'

'God knows, I just do. Where's Max?'

'Do you mean, how're things between us or where is he?'

I laughed. 'Both.'

'Things are fine. He's out checking up on Sean Beckett. Apparently he hasn't been seen around his usual haunts for the past few days. Max wants to keep tabs on him.'

'Good idea. Well, you've got the address in Wollstonecraft. I guess we meet there at eight fifty-five or thereabouts and go on in.'

'Do you remember the layout? I'm thinking of the wheelchair.'

I considered. 'A few steps. Nothing we can't handle.'

'My heroes. I'll see you there, Cliff.'

Which left me with most of a day to fill in. I drove to the office and dealt with the matters that had accumulated over the time I'd been concentrating on the Beckett case. It was clear from the answering machine messages and faxes that I'd missed out on some business in that time. I chased up some of the people who'd faxed and called and made some appointments—with a dentist who wanted some overdue accounts pursued, with a widow who claimed her late husband had been sighted in Vanuatu and with a gambler who wanted an escort to and from the Sydney Casino in the next week.

Bob Lowenstein had faxed his account, minutely itemised and ludicrously small. Appropriate really, considering that I'd been working for free for the past few days. He attached a note asking to be brought up to date and declaring his willingness to have 'professional intercourse' with Peggy Hawkins if such was needed. As a 'complimentary service' he'd run the name Claudia Vardon through every relevant database he could think of and had come up with nothing. I wasn't surprised. I wrote him a cheque and promised to stay in touch.

I dug out the contract I'd signed with Barry White and read through its provisions with growing amusement. With all its handwritten and initialled amendments and corrections, it wasn't worth the match it'd take to burn it. Something for the files. I leaned back in my chair and allowed my mind to play on the question of the reward for information leading to the conviction of those responsible for the death of Ramona Beckett. A million dollars or so. Somehow I didn't feel that the things I'd been doing had brought me any closer to it. Maybe I was even further away.

I drove home keeping an eye out for 4WDs and blondes and brunettes in dark glasses. I showered again and shaved again but I didn't go for the suit. I put on jeans and my old Italian slip-ons, strapped the shoulder holster on over a blue cotton shirt and laid out a light cotton jacket. With the way this case had been going I could be sitting all night in the parlour with my legs crossed or thrashing around in the bushes of Mrs Beckett's mansion. I put the .38 on the kitchen sink and used the jaffle-maker my sister had given me to build a giant construction crammed with all the leftovers in the fridge. I permitted myself one glass of wine and then extended the permit to two.

That got me through to a bit before seven with still a long time to wait. I deliberated about the gun but decided to take it. I considered ringing Frank Parker and decided not to. The front door-bell rang and I swore, then got cautious. I picked up the gun and held it behind my back as I opened the door after first switching on the outside light.

The woman who stood there was tall and straight. Her black hair fell to her shoulders and her make-up accentuated the size of her dark eyes, the sharp planes of her face and the wide slash of her mouth. She wore high heels, a short black leather skirt, a white blouse with a leather jerkin over it and a jacket to match.

'Hi, Cliff. Going to invite me in again?'

The voice was Claudia Vardon's, but the face and body were those of Ramona Beckett.

24

I stood aside and let her in. I forgot about the gun and she saw it as I closed the door.

'You won't need that,' she said.

'With you, there's no knowing.'

She walked ahead of me down the hall. Her legs were perfect and her carriage was beautiful. I recalled that Ramona Beckett had been a gymnast and I remembered how this woman had flicked herself up and off the bed in her apartment. I was well on the way to believing her and I forced myself to pull back. Dyed hair or a wig, make-up and clothes can work miracles, they can even change a man into a simulacrum of a woman. She looked around the living room and turned towards me, smiling. Nothing about her was familiar except the black leather shoulder bag. She threw it at the chair with the same result as before.

'A dump, but a nice dump. Could I have a drink, Cliff? I haven't had one for days. I've lost a few pounds, wouldn't you say?'

I put the gun away in the closet and took

off the holster. Guns weren't relevant here. 'You're a bit thinner,' I said. 'Why?'

'Gabriella notices such things. She puts store in them. I'm nine kilos heavier than when she last saw me, but every little bit helps.'

I poured two glasses which emptied the bottle. We'd have to go on to Scotch if there was to be any more drinking. The experience was very peculiar. I didn't know whether I was dealing with the woman I'd made love to seventeen years ago in a Potts Point flat, or another woman who'd slept with me right here just a few days before. She wanted me to believe it was both, but she'd have to prove it. She was sitting down now, showing flawless knees, calves and ankles under the short skirt. I handed her the glass, put a blank tape in the stereo set-up and switched it to pick up what was said in the room.

'OK?' I said.

'Why not?'

I hit Record and backed away to stand by the window.

'I'm Ramona Beckett,' she said.

'So you say.'

'You doubt it?'

I took a drink, put the glass down, made a frame with my fingers and looked through it. 'Start with the head,' I said brutally. 'The features are a bit different. Not as sharp. You seem to have perfect teeth. Ramona's weren't her best feature.'

She frowned. 'You're a bastard. You're talking about seventeen years and a car accident. That wasn't true what I told you. They had to remodel my nose, mouth and jaw. I always thought they did a good job.' She tapped her glass against her white teeth. 'I gave up smoking twelve years ago. My teeth were yellow by then. Anyway, these have been capped and veneered at great expense.'

I shrugged. 'I'm not convinced.'

'I should be able to remember the name of that fancy Italian restaurant you took me to when you were pretending to be Peter McIntrye, who could pick the Liberal candidate for the seat of Bligh, but I can't. We went back to my place in Potts Point and fucked our brains out. I remember that, kind of. Then you got busy and really screwed me, with that videotape switch and all.'

'I told that, more or less, to Barry White. You could've got it from him. Or . . .'

'Or what?'

'From Ramona Beckett, if you were involved in her kidnapping.'

Rather than crossing her legs or playing those kinds of games, she leaned forward earnestly in the chair towards me. 'There was no kidnapping, Cliff. I faked the whole damn thing.'

She told me that she had lost interest in getting into politics after I'd turned the tables on her. She'd accumulated a fair bit of money but she'd also acquired a cocaine habit and wanted more. She went to Manly and allowed herself to be seen, arranged things just so in her flat, sent a note to her parents' house and went to ground.

'Where?' I asked.

'Melbourne, where else? No-one in Melbourne cares about what's happening in Sydney and vice versa. I changed my appearance, cut the hair, ditched the leather. I'd opened a bank account in a false name and I waited for the money to come in.'

'The note was a newspaper cut-out job, right?'

'No. It was typed by me on an IBM Selectric that's now at the bottom of the harbour around from Mrs Macquarie's Chair.'

'Go on.'

'I couldn't believe it when the money wasn't paid. I mean I hated them and I knew they hated me, but . . .'

'Hold on, do you mean your father and mother or just Sean and Estelle?'

'The whole lot of them! My father was a pig! He raped Estelle, that's why his first wife left him. But he had the money to make it too hard for her to do anything about it. He tried it with me but Gabrielle stopped him. Don't think she was protecting me—she was just jealous.'

'This is all hard to believe. Joshua Beckett put up a big reward.'

'Sure. That made him look good, didn't it? And don't tell me investing it made it any more serious. He was probably just so busy making money in other directions that he forgot to pull the reward money out before he died.'

'Proof,' I said. 'Some proof.'

She stood, took off her jacket and draped it over the back of the chair. The sleeves of her silk blouse were loose and caught at the wrists, a style Ramona Beckett had favoured. She took two steps towards me and put out her right hand. 'I haven't got any moles or birthmarks as you very well know, but take hold of my hand.'

Against my better judgment I did.

'Do you remember the first thing you said to me when we met in that restaurant?'

I shook my head. I was still holding her hand.

'You said, "Your hand's so cold, Ramona". You remarked on it afterwards, too, when I grabbed your cock.'

Impossible to forget. I remembered that her touch was icy. But this woman's was many degrees warmer.

'Your hand's not cold.'

'It was the drugs. I was on so many things.'

She broke the contact and sat down. 'Still not convinced?'

'Go on with the story,' I said. I glanced at my watch. 'We've got a bit of time. That's if you're really planning to come to Wollstone-craft.'

'Of course I'm coming! This is harder than I thought it'd be. I get the feeling you've never changed in your whole life. That you've always been this hard, cynical type with just enough of a sense of humour to make you human.'

I finished my wine and thought about the Scotch. 'What's that got to do with anything?'

'I changed, Cliff. I really did. Holed-up in that dump in St Kilda, I really hit rock bottom. First thing was I got hold of some really bad coke. I'd been used to the very best stuff up here and this was dreadful. God knows what it was cut with but it nearly sent me nuts. So, of course, I decided to get off it. Have you ever used coke, Cliff?'

'No.'

'Wise man. Don't. And don't let anyone tell you it's not addictive. In a pig's eye it isn't. I had the worst time and it wasn't helped by my knowing that no-one in my family thought I was worth . . .'

'How much?'

'Two hundred grand. Not a hell of a lot. I had that much and more already. God, I suppose I was testing them in the only way I knew how. Hey, I'm not asking for sympathy here. I'm just trying to be accurate, all right?'

'The amount checks out,' I said quietly. 'But you could still have got that from Ramona herself.'

'Yes, I suppose so. Well, I guess you won't be convinced until Gabriella gives me the nod.'

'You use her first name.'

'Always did. You'll see. Are you going to tell me who intercepted the note and thought it was OK for me to go down where I put the typewriter?'

I'd felt tension building up in my body from the moment she'd arrived. It was partly sexual, of course, she was putting out the kinds of signals Ramona had, but now I was confused because Claudia's flags had spelled out pretty much the same message. But it could still all have been a carefully constructed act.

'Is that what this is all about?'

'What else? That's why I came back. That's why you and I are here like this. I know you've been to see Leo Grogan so you've got an idea of how I started out. I knew from painful experience that you were good at what you did, Cliff. I knew you'd be able to dig up the truth if you had a little help.'

'You hated me,' I said. As soon as I spoke I realised that the statement was an implicit acceptance of her story. I couldn't take it back, but I could watch her reaction closely.

'I don't hate you any more,' she said. 'We'd better go, hadn't we?'

I didn't learn anything from that. She put her empty glass on the nearest flat surface, stood and shrugged back into her jacket. She did it matter-of-factly enough, but that only made the erotic touches—the rise of her breasts and the athletic flex of her shoulders—all the more emphatic. At that moment I didn't care who she was, Ramona, Claudia, Madonna. I just wanted her physically the way an adolescent wants the first girl who'll let him touch her inside her clothes. But I was a long way past adolescence. I hooked my own jacket from the stair post.

'I'll tell you what you want to know when I'm convinced,' I said.

'Fair enough.'

'And when Max and Penny are convinced.'

'No fair.'

'You've spent too long in America.'

'You're right. Your car or mine?'

I stopped the tape and removed the cassette. 'Both,' I said.

She was driving a Falcon about twenty years younger than mine and I only saw her for the first few minutes. She drove fast, quickly leaving me behind and I was happy to tootle along trying to make sense of what she'd told me. It held together reasonably well if you accepted certain of her propositions—the dysfunctional nature of the family, her drug habit and its aftermath—but it certainly needed more glue. Why had she gone to the States and why had she stayed? More importantly, why had she come back and taken this tortuous route to enlightenment?

She was standing outside the Beckett place when I drew up. I sucked in a breath at the sight of her, alluring in the black leather with a street light a little further down the road giving her a long, slender shadow. A high-top taxi pulled up and Max and Penny went through their routine. I stood beside the leather-clad woman and watched.

'Are they an item?' she said.

'As of today.'

'That's nice. Max and Penny, right?'

'Right. Max is stone deaf but he won't have any trouble following you if he can see your mouth.'

'Can he sign?'

'What?'

The wheelchair was purring towards us now

and she waited until it was close before moving into the patch of light and making gestures with her hands. Max stopped abruptly. The wheelchair kept going for a few metres before Penny stopped it. Max was moving his hands as if he was knitting.

'She speaks sign,' Max said. 'Is this Claudia Vardon?'

'Ramona Beckett,' she said. 'I only know a little bit. Polite stuff.'

Penny watched with a frozen face as they exchanged a few more signs. She swivelled around and looked at me. 'Who is she?'

I shrugged. 'She says she's Ramona Beckett.'

'Do you believe her?'

'I want to see what Mrs Beckett says. A mother should know, wouldn't you say?'

Max had regained his composure. He extended a hand and he and Claudia/Ramona shook formally. 'This is Penny Draper, Ms Vardon,' he said. 'Where did you learn to sign?'

'In a very good hospital in California. They did everything to rehabilitate accident victims— Braille, sign . . .'

'Are we going in, Cliff?' Penny said. 'It's cold out here for those of us without thousand-dollar leather jackets.'

25

After getting the all-clear at the gate, Max and I manhandled the wheelchair up the steps to the house. The small dark woman let us in and we wheeled and trooped through to the room where Gabriella Beckett and Wallace Cavendish had received me before. Max and Penny went in first and I followed. Mrs Beckett was sitting in the same chair, wearing the same dress and expression. Cavendish had changed almost out of recognition. His hair and suit, both formerly immaculate, were rumpled and his striped club tie was askew.

Mrs Beckett reached into the bag on her lap and took out a pair of silver-rimmed spectacles. She put them on and scanned the group of visitors.

'Where is she?'

I hadn't noticed but the woman in leather had hung back and not entered the room. Now she came striding in with her shoulder bag almost swinging.

'Here I am, Gabriella, and here's something

for you.' She stepped up close and dropped something in Mrs Beckett's lap.

Mrs Beckett's fingers fumbled for a second, then she held up a tiny gold locket on a thin chain. 'Oh, god, Ramona. It's you.'

'You gave me that on my tenth birthday. Inside is a picture of my grandfather. You said he was the best man you ever knew. I've wondered all my life what you meant by that. Will you tell me now?'

Mrs Beckett came up out of her chair but the woman claiming to be her daughter stepped back.

'None of that. It's way too late.'

Mrs Beckett slumped back into her chair and slid the chain through her fingers. I was aware of what a brilliant strategy it was for someone in Ramona/Claudia's position to present an item and pose a question. Too clever perhaps, I was still sceptical.

'You are cruel, Ramona,' Mrs Beckett murmured. 'You were always cruel.'

'I learned it right here. Hello, Wallace, you prick.'

Cavendish just stared at her, unable to speak. She turned away from them and faced us, Max, Penny and me. 'I phoned Wallace this morning and gave him a description of our last fuck. Chapter and verse. That's why he was so obliging to you, Cliff. How about we all sit down? Christ, I need to. I haven't worn heels this high in years.'

Penny took that as her cue. She was already sitting down. While the rest of us squatted she wheeled up close to Mrs Beckett. 'I'm Penny

Draper, Mrs Beckett. I'm a consultant detective with the New South Wales Police Force. Do you acknowledge this woman as your daughter, Ramona Louise Beckett?'

'I do, yes. She is Ramona.'

'How can you be sure?' Penny pressed. 'If she was one of the people who kidnapped your daughter she could have extracted the story about the locket from her. She's gone to great length with her appearance. Are you sure this isn't a very clever impersonation?'

'I'm sure.'

'Why?'

'Her eyes. She has my father's eyes. Don't ask me to explain it, but I have never seen any other human being with such eyes.'

'Contacts,' Penny said.

Mrs Beckett shook her head. 'No.'

Max spoke for the first time. 'This is easily decided. Ramona Beckett was twice convicted of driving offences. Her fingerprints are on file. Would you consent to a comparison, Ms ... Vardon?'

She laughed and Mrs Beckett and Cavendish exchanged anguished glances at the sound. I knew what they were thinking. Ramona Beckett's laugh was utterly distinctive, a pure peal, and this was it.

'The voice of reason,' she said, facing Max directly. 'Max, I'd be glad to oblige. Got your ink pad with you? Urine sample, blood test, DNA. Whatever you like.'

Cavendish evidently felt he'd been out of the

action too long. 'This is Ramona Beckett, Hardy,' he said. 'Older and heavier, but no doubt about it.'

'Thank you for nothing,' she said. 'And I don't think you need to say another word until you're asked. Cliff, convinced?'

Two could play at deflective strategies. 'I wonder if we could have something to drink, Mrs Beckett?' I said. 'I think we could be in for a long session.'

'Certainly. Call Nora would you, Wallace?'

'What happened to Nolan?'

Mrs Beckett's head tilted a little, her fine dark eyes swept over us and her reply was directed at us all. 'The butler,' she said. 'Ramona hated him. He died.'

'Good. I did hate him. You're right.'

Cavendish left the room and I wondered whether he'd come back. I was pretty convinced by now but I wasn't going to throw in the towel completely. 'I'd like to hear some more about what you did ... what you *say* you did after the kidnapping stunt failed.'

Ramona gripped the thick, black hair at the crown of her head and pulled. The wig came free. Her own hair was curled in a bun at the back. She released it and let the white mane flow freely. Mrs Beckett's gasp was audible. Ramona looked ten years older without the wig but her mother seemed to have aged twenty years.

'Reminds you of how old you are, doesn't it, Gabriella?'

Mrs Beckett didn't answer but she looked

relieved when Cavendish and the servant came in, both carrying trays. Cavendish poured Hennessy brandy over ice for himself and Mrs Beckett, added a splash of soda, gave her the drink and took his back to his seat. Nora served the rest of us—whisky for Max and me, brandy for Penny. Ramona had a small glass of neat vodka.

'I've already told Cliff about faking the kidnapping. I was hiding in Melbourne. I had some bad cocaine and then a very hard time getting off drugs. I was disgusted with my family and even more disgusted with myself, with what I'd been doing. I had half a dozen bank accounts and two passports. I just upped stakes and went to America.'

'What happened to your beautiful hair?' Mrs Beckett said.

Ramona sipped her vodka. 'You are the most superficial person I've ever met. Appearances are all that matter to you, all that ever mattered. As long as I was the prettiest girl in the school everything was fine. The fact that I was the most intelligent didn't mean shit. The hair? I was in an auto accident. I broke some bones and my hair went white. I was pregnant. I lost the baby, but that wouldn't matter to you, would it?'

'Oh, Ramona . . .' Mrs Beckett was half out of her chair again but her daughter's fierce look drove her back.

'That's it,' Ramona said. 'That's all you need to know. Now what I want to know is, who suppressed my note? Who paid off the police? Who wanted me dead?' She finished her drink and looked at Cavendish. 'I know you had a hand in it, Wallace. I can smell it. Did you know that, Gabriella? That your trusted legal adviser connived at the murder of your daughter? Or did the note only get as far as you anyway? Or was it Papa? Old big dick? Maybe him and Estelle? They were *close*. Weren't they, Gabriella? Maybe Sean, who knew I knew he liked diddling little boys? Huh?'

Mrs Beckett shook her head and didn't speak.

It was Penny who broke the silence that followed Ramona's statement. She moved her wheelchair back and forth a little and the movement attracted everyone's attention. I suspected it was a trick she'd used before. 'I believe you're Ramona Beckett,' she said. 'I believe that you did as you say you did. That makes you guilty of public mischief, passport violations and probably other things. You contributed to the corruption of several police officers as well, but that's all small beer and old news. I want to know why you've come back, and you're not going to learn what you want to know from Cliff or Max or me until you tell us what you plan to do with the information.'

Ramona looked at me. 'You did the leg work, Cliff. Ten thousand for the name or names.'

I shook my head.

She turned to look at Cavendish. 'Wallace'll tell me for a blow job.'

Cavendish removed the show handkerchief from the pocket of his suit coat and wiped his face. 'You're disgusting.'

Colour flooded into Ramona's face and she clenched both fists. I thought for a second that she'd attack Cavendish in some way, verbal or physical, but she visibly fought for control. She relaxed her hands and took one deep breath, then several more, then she closed her eyes and dropped her head. It looked like some kind of ritual. She lifted her head and she was looking straight at me. 'Remember the way I was, Cliff? Seventeen years ago?'

'I remember.'

'What would you expect my motive to be, if I was still like that?'

'Revenge,' I said.

'Right. Well, it's not so. I've been in therapy for quite a few years now. My therapist saw that I had a great deal of anger inside me, an unhealthy amount. I was running on anger and not much more. It puzzled her because of course I hadn't told her the truth about me. Eventually, I did tell her the truth. The whole goddamn story.'

As she talked the stiffness left her body and the aggression went out of her voice. As her features relaxed, aggression was replaced by confidence and composure. I wondered what sort of effort it took to effect this transformation and how long it could be kept in place. I was still sceptical but also confused. The beating she'd arranged for me and the lies and the manipulation were the work of Ramona. This was Claudia again and I remembered making love with her—the warmth of her mouth and the smoothness of her skin. There was no million dollars and I didn't care.

There was only her, and no-one else in the room mattered to me. Her words, *I don't hate you any more*, were whispering inside my head.

'That's very interesting, Ms Beckett,' Penny said. 'But you haven't answered the question.'

'I'm not interested in revenge or a pound of flesh,' Ramona said. 'My husband, the father of the child I lost, was killed as well. He was rich and now I'm rich, too.'

'Good for you,' Penny said. 'That makes three rich people in this room and three poor ones. The poor ones want an answer to the question.'

'Ramona,' Mrs Beckett said. 'Your father died believing that you had been abducted and murdered. Until today I believed it too.'

'Good, Gabriella. That's good.'

Penny shifted impatiently in her wheelchair and opened her mouth to speak.

I interrupted. 'What's the answer, Claudia?'

She smiled at me. 'It's a nice name, isn't it? The answer is that I have to know who it was who hated me that much so that I can forgive that person. So that I can tell him or her that it's over. All finished, forgiven and forgotten. That's all. And I'll be doing it for utterly selfish reasons—for me, not for him or her.'

Cavendish gave a derisive snort. 'I don't believe you.'

'I think I do,' I said. 'Sean suppressed the note. With Cavendish's help he paid off the police. I suspect that Cavendish has been blackmailing him ever since.'

'Thank you, Cliff,' Ramona Beckett said.

26

Cavendish, Bryce and Lane sent me a cheque that more than covered all my expenses in the Ramona Beckett matter. A note from Mrs Horsfield said that the firm was acting under instruction from some corporation I'd never heard of. I banked the cheque and rang Wallace Cavendish. He told me that Ramona had left the country two days after our meeting. He was no longer acting for Mrs Beckett. His last service for her had been to draw up a will in which certain charities nominated by her daughter were beneficiaries. Ramona had threatened her mother that, if she attempted to name her in the will, she would publish every last detail about the family's misfortunes.

Cavendish was still acting for Sean Beckett who, he told me, had had a long meeting with his half-sister. Ramona had made absolutely no demands on him other than to make him promise not to divulge anything about her to anyone.

Max chafed at being unable to close out the Beckett case but he saw that there was no way to do it. Neither Mrs Beckett nor Sean Beckett nor

Cavendish would offer support to any report he might prepare. Me, either. He had his consolation—he and Penny were married about a month after the business finished. Colin Sligo was dead by then. Bob Lowenstein reported to me that Satisfaction was still going strong under the able management of Peggy Hawkins.

I checked out a loose end in the person of Leo Grogan to see if he had any whiff of what might have really been behind his meetings with the mystery woman and Barry White. He couldn't have cared less. He'd got some kind of a compensation payment for his accident and was steadily drinking it and his life away.

Sometimes I see a dark woman in black leather in the street and I catch my breath. Or I glimpse a woman with a mane of white hair and the same thing happens. I've even been known to follow them for a block or two, but they never turn out to be Ramona Beckett or Claudia Vardon. I never saw either of them again.

THE WASHINGTON CLUB
A Cliff Hardy Novel
by Peter Corris

Claudia Fleischman is beautiful, rich, intelligent . . . and has just been charged with the murder of her developer husband.

Hardy, hired to look into the background of the case, is soon up to his neck in trouble. When his car is blown up and then a friend is killed, Cliff finds himself with a personal stake in the action. His investigations introduce him to the shadowy world of corporate high fliers at Sydney's exclusive Washington Club and bring him into contact with loose cannon 'Haitch' Henderson and his soft but unpleasant pimp of a son, Noel.

In one of his grittiest cases ever, Hardy has to take drastic action before the pieces fall into place and a very rough justice is seen to be done.

BANTAM BOOKS
ISBN: 0 73380 031 9

FORGET ME IF YOU CAN
Cliff Hardy Stories
by Peter Corris

Even when he's not involved in a major case, PI Cliff Hardy's life is far from routine.

In these stories, a whistleblower is himself betrayed, a son turns against his father, brothers feud, men are harassed by women, and things are never quite what they seem . . . Whether on the familiar streets of Sydney or out of town, Hardy's cases don't always have tidy endings—and sometimes he has to take the law into his own hands.

BANTAM BOOKS
ISBN: 0 73380 066 1